The Consequence of Sex

Also by Robert C. Reinhart:

Novels

A History of Shadows
Beldon's Crimes
Walk the Night

Drama

Telling Moments: 15 Gay Monologues

Nonfiction

The Cramped Quarters Cookbook
A Concise Chronology of American Movies

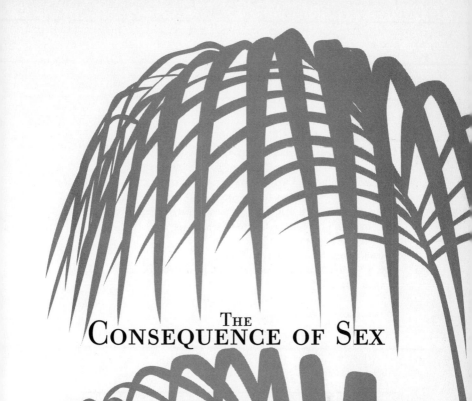

THE
CONSEQUENCE OF SEX

By Robert C. Reinhart

alyson books
los angeles

MANUFACTURED IN THE UNITED STATES OF AMERICA.

THIS TRADE PAPERBACK ORIGINAL IS PUBLISHED ALYSON PUBLICATIONS,
P.O. BOX 4371, LOS ANGELES, CALIFORNIA 90078-4371.
DISTRIBUTION IN THE UNITED KINGDOM BY
TURNAROUND PUBLISHER SERVICES LTD.,
UNIT 3, OLYMPIA TRADING ESTATE, COBURG ROAD, WOOD GREEN,
LONDON N22 6TZ ENGLAND.

FIRST EDITION: NOVEMBER 2003

03 04 05 06 07 **a** 10 9 8 7 6 5 4 3 2 1

ISBN 1-55583-772-7

LIBRARY OF CONGRESS CATALOGING-IN-PUBLICATION DATA
  REINHART, ROBERT C.
    THE CONSEQUENCE OF SEX / BY ROBERT C. REINHART.—1ST ED.
    ISBN 1-55583-772-7
      1. GAY MEN—FICTION. I. TITLE.
  PS3568.E4924C66 2003
  813'.54—DC21   2003052420

CREDITS
• "MURDER" IS AN EDITED EXCERPT FROM THE NOVEL *BELDON'S CRIMES*,
ALYSON, © 1986 BY ROBERT C. REINHART. "ACTOR" IS AN EDITED EXCERPT
FROM THE NOVEL *A HISTORY OF SHADOWS*, AVON, © 1982 BY ROBERT C.
REINHART.
• COVER PHOTOGRAPH OF MEN EMBRACING BY ROBERTA ROMA. COVER PHO-
TOGRAPH OF PALM TREES FROM STONE/MARK HARRIS.
• COVER DESIGN BY MATT SAMS.

This book is for the many friends whose stories I've cribbed. Some are gone, and discretion tells me that the others would probably prefer I shut up about who they are. This book is also for a remarkably durable friend, Jim Peacock, and for my nephew Gary Amell.

In the ninth grade sex got a death grip on boys' crotches. They passed around crudely printed pornography and their jokes became exclusively about sex, while something inside me stood apart and could only observe, because I had absolutely no idea why girls were supposed to excite me.

—"Clifford" by Robert C. Reinhart

Contents

The Boys of Mérida

Mr. Tunsmith always went to Mérida in January, not driven there by California's rains so much as by the memory of Mérida's beauties. He was not tugged there by the elegance of the Zócalo, with its game board of geometrically sculpted trees, nor by the stateliness of the buildings that bordered that park on all sides and evoked the native's ancestral Spain as strongly as the aroma of paella. Nor did he go to view and consider the tantalizing mysteries of the nearby Mayan ruins, nor for the soul-softening sound of fountains in coolly shadowed courtyards. After all, his native Los Angeles had courtyards and fountains and fanciful simulations of every architectural structure known to man, even ruins, though recently built ones. What carried Mr. Tunsmith to Mérida and what he cared about desperately—achingly—were the young men of Mérida; young men the color of strong tea, with teeth as white and hard as Meissen and skin that whispered and flowed under his fingertips like sun-soaked marble, telling him the secrets of blood so many degrees warmer than his own. Touching the boys drove California's January damp from his bones and gave him enough stirringly durable memories to let him weather another heart-cooling year of air conditioning in his Los Angeles beauty shop.

Every year he would delay shopping for his vacation wardrobe until September, postponing this pleasure with a great effort of will, like a determined dieter who endures a lawnful of lawful lettuce before sinking from sight into a hot fudge sundae. Food and wardrobe had become commingled, as each year increased his burden of weight and birthdays. He didn't mind the weight too much; he felt his now-considerable size gave him "substance," a presence he felt he'd lacked as a thin young thing. Then, too, his increasing ampleness lent timbre to his once-light voice, and it now reverberated up from his mass like low notes from an oboe, rather than whistling reedily out as it had when he was more flutelike. While some of his peers had remained determinedly thin and grown wrinkled as used tissue paper, he saw, as he squinted into his bathroom mirror, that his hoarded pounds made his face as smooth as a teenager's. All he hated about his gathered girth was that it made his privates less visible—made his privates more *private*, as he joked to himself. Lately, in an effort to ease his discomfort at the apparent diminishing of this once-proud feature, he took to thinking of it as decorative, as a corsage of small pink buds—which, indeed, it resembled.

Mr. Tunsmith always stayed at Mérida's Hotel Casa del Sol at Calle 60. It stood near parks full of young men who found they had a value far beyond any they had been led to imagine by their families, teachers, or the Catholic Church. From prepubescence on, priests had whispered hot warnings at them through the confessional grills about the eternal roasting they would suffer for "spending seed," a phrase innocuously remote from the delights of masturbation. So roundabout were the priests in dealing with the sultry subject of sex that the boys of Mérida went innocently into the arms of the "rich" male and female Americans who flocked to their town.

Most of the Americans claimed they came on cultural pilgrimages to contemplate a lost Mayan civilization. Some did. Many more were intent on investigating the biological changes time and cavorting with Spanish invaders had wrought on the Mayan anatomy.

In their own way, the Americans equally fascinated the boys of Mérida. The boys couldn't imagine why these Americans spent days trekking across hot dusty plains fending off hoards of souvenir sellers just to look at the messy remains of their ancestors' villages. What the boys longed to see were the wondrously practical electronic mansions these Americans had foolishly left. How could these people care for ruins when they had rock and roll and a hundred channels of television and every food in the world could be bought in their supermarkets? How could they be impressed with heaps of masonry when they could ride in immense cars to buy anything they desired and without a thought about what it cost? The boys were even slightly bemused about why these bewildering tourists chose to pour gold over their naked bodies and feed them as lavishly as their ancestral priests had once fed human offerings. Still, experience told the boys they had value, and after so many years of tourists, they were able to calculate this value precisely.

Theirs wasn't a bad life at all; it felt good, required little effort, and there was nothing they could see in their futures that held half the comforts of the present. And the price of this good life? Nothing, really. Only the temporary use of their bodies, which, put to laboring, would have earned them the barest subsistence.

While most tourists were birds of a single season, Mr. Tunsmith's annual arrival made him legendary among the boys of the park. He was handed down through their short generations of desirability so that, after only 15 years, he was now meeting their fifth generation, former generations having grown overripe for the life, or married, or grown too used, or—the rare, envied, and fortunate few—been "adopted" by pale Americano patrons.

New boys always heard about Mr. Tunsmith. As Fernando was telling that year's recruits in December, "You just wait. Mr. Tunsmith is the best. And reliable. Every January. And generous. See this ring? Real gold. And enough pesos for Mama's refrigerator last year. And good clothes so he can take us to restaurants and we can look just like everyone else there. I'll introduce you to him. I'm one of his favorites. Good times coming in January. Rich times. My Mr. Tunsmith is coming."

But even with the ever-weakening peso, the coming January was going to be a strain on Mr.

Tunsmith's resources, so, instead of shopping for his wardrobe in Robinson's and Bonwit's, he sought less luxurious sources, ending by buying two white suits and two pairs of white trousers at Bernie's Big Man's Budget Boutique and treating himself to orchid, crimson, and orange shirts, with almost-matching silk pocket handkerchiefs from Robinson's. Last year's white shoes would just have to do, as would last season's silk underwear.

He couldn't save on the hotel, because he couldn't bring himself to ask for a cheaper room. He felt that nothing less than their best room and large, silencing tips could guarantee afternoons of uninterrupted pleasure. What would the boys think of him in a cramped room? They'd smell his poorer circumstances or think he'd grown mean-spirited. So he counted pennies and, for the first time, made a budget, though it made him feel stingy to think of skimping on the boys who gave him a whole year's worth of remembered pleasures. There would be no small tributes of gold this year for his favorites, but there could be lavish gifts of silver. Well, fairly lavish.

He followed the course of the peso in the *Los Angeles Times,* his mood rising or falling disproportionately with the volatile currency. Every night as he ate his large ration of hamburgers in a drive-in he couldn't help but think that this wretched, if plentiful, mess cost almost as much as lunch for four at the lovely and excellent La Gondola in Mérida, even with the bottles of wine that made the boys so woozily amiable and sweet. And instead of eating alone in his car, he would have their enchanting company on a shadowed patio at a table glowing with snowy linen.

He finished his dinner by using the remaining fries to scour the last of the ketchup from the limp paper plate, and then drove slowly home, in no hurry to get there, because all there was to do was watch the soap operas his VCR had saved that afternoon.

It had been years since he had driven through Los Angeles's hustler haunts or went to the gay bars or baths. At forty-seven he felt that whatever charms and excitements those places had once held were as long gone as his own allure. Besides, it felt particularly awful to be old and unattractive in a city where everybody's tanned skin seemed to fit so well. It was best to slip from sight when one became less than wonderful to behold. If he had the money to buy a newly cosmeticized exterior, he might have lived more years in public. So, some years ago, Mr. Tunsmith had gradually retired to X-rated videotapes and masturbation, until even these seemed nearly pointless. But it was more than his own appearance that kept him out of the cruising parks and streets. It was also the stories he had heard over the years from his older friends of beatings and robberies and the cruelty of the police.

He might have made more money at his beauty shop if he'd tried, but his days of striving ended when he reached a level of comfort that suited him. He remained a brilliant, if disinterested, hairstylist. Still, his shop had slid with the neighborhood, descending with the inexorable slowness of a frigid mudslide, riding down with the declining fortunes of the area.

He had opened his shop twenty-two years ago in a lovely, well-tended neighborhood, and as some of his customers' fortunes carried them up in the world they urged him to follow them into increasing affluence. He didn't because, in a way, he had come to hate heads and hair. A rich scalp was as repellent to him as a poor one. So, he patched the tears in the customer chairs with Mystic tape, replaced aging plate glass mirrors with cheap ones that made reflections wobble. He didn't even bother replacing ailing equipment, just let it screech and grind on till it started blowing fuses. After all, the mechanical complaints of the equipment weren't any worse than the clattery rock music his present customers preferred. His present customers didn't want excellence; they wanted something like the pictures they clipped from cheap magazines that showed baroquely overwrought styles teetering above pampered ferocious faces. He often reached such a pitch of disaffection with his work and felt so vindictive that he would take the spun-sugar style requested and elevate it to an apex of coiling ugliness. He was making a comment, but they missed his irony and loved what he did, even if it lasted only a few hours before settling on their heads like slain birds.

All in all, things were pretty bad, but nobody had to tell him that, and even if they had, he wouldn't have minded much. Even the chocolates he munched all day had gone from the jewel box elegance of Godiva to the economy-size carton of Milk Duds.

But there was a remedy for his soul in Mérida, and he got through the rigorous hours of arranging

December's holiday hair by gazing beyond the glazed faces in the mirror to a landscape in his mind where the boys of Mérida stood waiting and smiling and promising.

He always arrived in Mérida on the evening of January third, timing it to minimize his chance of being seen unshaven, rumpled, and still damp with fear from his flight. His wardrobe would be put immediately into the hands of the staff for refurbishing before he fell exhausted onto his bed to rest and anticipate his entrance the next day. He knew that after all these years his arrival was now something of a tradition for the boys, and he tried to keep it fresh for his audience. It made him feel special when he saw their welcoming faces, and he knew for the first time in months that he was where he belonged, was home. If he could have put a name to his feelings, it would have been *safe*. He knew the boys were eager for the food and money and jewelry and that each would tell him some sad tale when they could get him alone. They would ask for money, but none had ever asked for more than was in his power to give, and it thrilled him to be able to be bountiful in ways that, while they were fairly small expenses for him, solved seemingly life-and-death problems for the boys.

He lay on his bed and foresaw his fifteenth entrance clearly. He would stroll down Calle 60 to arrive at the Zócalo promptly at one. He would enter the northeast corner of the park and saunter slowly around the park's perimeter. Then, as the mood took him, he would amble along the diagonal walkways, giving the impression that he was taking in the highly varied life there, but in fact, he would only be masking his anxiety while he waited for the first of his young friends to come greet him.

The honor of greeting him was usually left to the most senior of the boys, and sad experience had taught him that this boy would probably be missing next year, having moved on to the hard adulthood of his poor country. So each year's greeting now held the poignancy of a final reunion.

Mr. Tunsmith arrived in the park promptly at 1 and began his stroll, moving sedately along the paths, trying hard to look the self-possessed master of all he surveyed, while his heart rang excitedly. He didn't notice the Mayan women in their white dresses with the splendid lace bottoms of their slips hanging inches below the hems. Nor did he see the gaggles of pretty schoolgirls in their sedate, sexless uniforms of blue, green, or brown. And he didn't notice the camera-bedecked tourists or the young couples who, as custom dictated, expressed public affection in the most circumspect of glances and touches. He didn't register the park's tailored greenery or the topiary or the lovely architecture. He barely noticed the multitude of halfhearted beggars who approached him and whose pleas he answered with a negative twitch of his head. Only his young friends mattered, only his boys. He had a lover's narrow vision where only the beloved filled the frame.

Within minutes he felt he had been in the park too

long. Was there no one left who remembered him? Was he being avoided? Where were his boys?

Across the Zócalo, Fernando grasped Carlos roughly by the shoulder and pointed, hissing, "There. Over there, you idiot. How can you miss someone that big?"

Carlos's head whipped from side to side until he saw the large figure in the blazingly white suit, crimson shirt, white tie, and red pocket handkerchief. Carlos's expression showed clearly that he was impressed by the sight, and this pleased Fernando, who had been telling Carlos for months that Mr. Tunsmith was exceptional, larger than life, a force, an immense benevolent act of God come to bless them all.

Carlos said with awe, "He's like a house, a big white house. My whole family could live there."

Fernando said irritably, "So what, he's rich."

"So many chins."

"He's rich."

"How does he find it to pee?"

"He's rich," Fernando persisted angrily. Carlos was an idiot to focus on physical irrelevancies.

"What will he want us to do? If he gets on top of me, he'll kill me."

"He might not want to do anything. Just shut your dumb mouth. He's good to us."

"How much do we ask?"

"We don't ask. He just gives. And more than the others. Run get that stupid Ramon and tell him to get his ass down here. He likes to eat and he's got a big dick. They'll both get what they want."

"But what do we do?"

"He'll take us for the best lunch you've ever had, you dumb peasant, and then he'll take us back to his air-conditioned room and we'll do this and that. On a full stomach and a little drunk. Get Ramon. Run!"

Fernando assumed leadership of the welcoming committee. When Carlos returned with Ramon, Fernando placed the shorter boys in front of him and, sensing the ceremonial gravity of the moment, waited with them at the end of the walk down which Mr. Tunsmith now came. Fernando kept stroking his neat hair into place, and he hissed at Carlos to push his shirttail in and take the Walkman's earphones off. He knocked Ramon on the shoulder and ordered him to stop twisting about.

Mr. Tunsmith saw the three waiting for him by the green bench and commanded himself to keep the excitement out of his face and walk slowly, to look the composed man of the world they would be expecting. He recognized the handsome Fernando but thought that, even at a distance, the other two looked charming—quite charming—and poignantly, tenderly young.

Fernando introduced Mr. Tunsmith to Carlos and Ramon with a deferential formality that lent the occasion such a sweet solemnity, it almost brought Mr. Tunsmith to tears. He found Fernando had matured amazingly in a year and looked very senior to the two boys with him. Was eleven months that long a time? Was this to be Fernando's last year in the park? Probably.

Mr. Tunsmith declared with a hectic enthusiasm he

couldn't control that he was delighted to meet Carlos and Ramon. Fernando translated Mr. Tunsmith's greetings in Spanish for the boys, who seemed indifferent to his professed delight and eyed him suspiciously. Mr. Tunsmith was now so excited and anxious to please—to launch his season in Mérida—that he didn't notice their indifference. Of course the day must be his treat, he told Fernando, assuming his young friends had the time to spare, and he so hoped they did. Might he take them shopping? Would they care for lunch afterward? It would give him the greatest pleasure to have their company, to treat them. And they must tell him all about themselves. Fernando must tell him all that had happened to him and his friends since last year.

They shopped the bustling length of Calle 58, with Mr. Tunsmith regulating their purchases to ensure that the clothes would be acceptable at La Gondola. He said no to T-shirts with logos of rock groups, but was otherwise so lavish with permission to spend that the boys became feverishly excited and grabbed at shirts and slacks and socks and anything, with no thought of size. Fernando was ashamed of them.

By three the excited group was being shown into the garden of La Gondola, which was almost empty, the American tourists to whom the restaurant catered long since gone.

Mr. Tunsmith helped them heap their parcels on the vacant chairs at the large table they were shown to and, acting the solicitous host, assigned them seats and said that, if the boys would permit, he would order for them all. Fernando translated. As to the wine, would something California do, or would they prefer a Spanish? Were his guests comfortable? He ordered from a bored waiter and then excused himself, moving into the dark interior of the restaurant to find the proprietor. He slipped the man a wad of pesos as he said, "So good to be back in your lovely restaurant. You'll be seeing a lot of me, as always. You always take such good care of me."

"So good to have you back, Mr. Tunsmith. You know you can always expect our best," the proprietor answered, trying to count the money in his hand by a kind of Braille.

Mr. Tunsmith returned to the table to find the boys bent intently over an excellent lime soup. They glanced up only to break bread off a large warm loaf. They ate with dedication. Carlos began to use his bread to whisk the soup bowl clean. Fernando said something sharp and Carlos snapped erect in his chair, looking irritated and puzzled as to why he should waste the glaze of soup that still coated his bowl.

Mr. Tunsmith barely understood a word said over lunch but didn't care. At Fernando's insistence, Carlos and Ramon tried their best to stick to their ragged English, but the least excitement—the sight of the next course, some remembered or unusual experience—carried them back into Spanish, where Mr. Tunsmith was happy to leave them. He was content to look at them and anticipate the hours ahead.

Mr. Tunsmith was listening to Fernando's lengthy account of his sister's wedding, when Carlos and

Ramon, who had been whispering, burst into an excited argument. Fernando furiously ordered them to be quiet and, after a flurry of argument, they all fell silent, Fernando glancing anxiously toward the restaurant to see if they'd been overheard.

Fernando made no effort to disguise his disgust with the boys. He said, "They are young and stupid, Mr. Tunsmith, and I apologize for them, because they're too dumb to apologize for themselves," a sentiment he repeated to the boys in snarling Spanish.

"No apology needed," Mr. Tunsmith said as he patted Fernando's hand, and to Carlos and Ramon he said slowly, "We are all good friends, are we not?"

"Not that one," Carlos said, aiming a sharp look at Ramon. Ramon snapped back and Fernando aimed a silencing look at them.

"What is it?" Mr. Tunsmith asked.

"Just more of their childish nonsense. And if they don't shut their dumb peasant faces, I'll send them both back to the park."

Mr. Tunsmith hated unpleasantness and knew how to keep boys happy. He asked, "Who'd like another dessert?"

"You're kind, Mr. Tunsmith," Fernando said, "but after so much wine, maybe we all need a siesta. I feel lazy," smiling and stretching sinuously. He turned to the other boys, saying sternly, "So do they." Fernando wanted them out of the restaurant before those two fools scared Mr. Tunsmith away.

As they moved through the restaurant Fernando hissed at Carlos and Ramon, "I introduce you to the best and you act like cheap whores. You shut up about that stuff. Hear me?"

The stuff they were to shut up about was the great current scandal driving the boys of the Zócalo to a fearful distrust of one another. Some among them were working with two policemen, not to abolish their trade but to capitalize on it. Boys would be reported in the rooms of tourists and the room would be raided. Money would then be extorted from the tourists, who were sweatily anxious to avoid prosecution. Then the tourists would be given the superfluous order to leave Mérida. But who was working with these policemen? And how long before other officials would want their share? Rampant greed could put them all out of business.

Fernando knew it was bad for business to have this news reach customers. Tourists should be kept calm and happy. That was just good business. Carlos and Ramon were stupid.

There was never more than one clerk on duty at the hotel's desk, and he sat under the protection of a balcony in the lushly planted interior courtyard. The rooms on the second and third floors led onto communal balconies, with access to the courtyard below by narrow stairways at both ends of the atrium.

Mr. Tunsmith led the way into the hotel and stopped at the desk, his large tip for the clerk already in hand. Fernando led Carlos and Ramon up the stairs to wait outside the room, while Mr. Tunsmith blinded the clerk with pesos. Mr. Tunsmith was babbling nervous pleasantries at the clerk, who was intently sliding the pile of notes toward himself.

This first moment of passage always jangled Mr. Tunsmith's nerves badly, so he didn't hear the two men as they came up to stand behind him. The young men took in the three boys climbing the stairs and Mr. Tunsmith's nervous bribery, and they exchanged a look under raised eyebrows that said this guy was crazy to have anything to do with underage peasant trade.

The young blond was trying to look around Mr. Tunsmith's shoulder to see how large the bribe was when, frightened by the man's unexpected presence behind him, Mr. Tunsmith whirled, knocking the blond man backward and sending the man's parcel crashing noisily to the floor. The sound of shattering glass came clearly through its brown wrapping paper.

Mr. Tunsmith's nerves broke with the glass and he babbled, "Oh, I'm so sorry. How clumsy of me. I didn't know you were so close. I want...I must pay for whatever..." but the anger on the blond's face cut his apology to shreds.

For a long moment the blond was too enraged to speak and could only glare at Mr. Tunsmith, who flapped his hands and stared fearfully at the deflated parcel on the flagstones. The dark-haired one of the pair laid a calming hand on the blond's shoulder and it was angrily shrugged off. The three boys on the balcony peered down and made Mr. Tunsmith feel even more ashamed.

The blond said, "Pay for it? *Pay for it?* It's one of a kind. There aren't any more. You can't pay for something that no longer exists. Don't you know that?"

Again the dark-haired one laid a hand on the blond's shoulder, and this time the blond knocked it off and said, "Mind your own business, Peter. I want this old fool to know..."

Now Peter was angry, but he knew better than to try and stop one of Derek's tirades. He stepped back. He was weary of Derek's rages. As usual, Derek had drunk too much over a too-long lunch and, as usual, they had argued and carried their parcel and their anger back to the hotel, again hoping to heal their antagonisms with sex, but Peter was getting weary of fucking to fix things. *We just do it to forget, never for fun,* Peter thought. More and more Peter was asking himself *What am I hanging on for?* and he was no longer even bothering to answer himself because he had ceased to care about an answer.

Without masking his disgust, Peter said, "I'm going to the room, Derek."

Peter moved away, leaving a surprised and deflated Derek. Why wasn't Peter trying to calm him as he always did? Something was suddenly different and wrong. And it was this fat old degenerate's fault. As much as he wanted to rail against this clumsy fool, following Peter was more pressing.

What was that tub of lard holding money toward him for? Did he really expect to pay for the lost treasure? The goblets were beyond price, and Derek would prove it by refusing the money. No, Derek would make his point of aesthetic superiority even stronger, and he did so by slapping the money from

Mr. Tunsmith's hand and stalking away, leaving the smashed parcel where it was.

Mr. Tunsmith gathered up the money and the crushed parcel, and carried both away, not daring to look at the room clerk.

The air conditioner in Mr. Tunsmith's room *brrred* while the ceiling fan—there more for picturesque effect than practicality—twirled languidly. The shutters on the window let blurred fingers of dusty light into the room, rendering the three naked young men on the bed tantalizingly out of focus. The trio moved smoothly over one another and, as Mr. Tunsmith leaned close to them, eager to see as much detail as possible in the dim light, he could hear the whisper of skin brushing skin and could separate the fan's hum from the sweetly happy sighs of the boys.

The boys were new to one another sexually. Always before, Carlos and Ramon had worked singly and had been carefully instructed by their employers as to what was expected, about what would please and what would not. Here they were not told what to do with one another.

When they had arrived in the room, Fernando had called Carlos and Ramon into the bathroom and explained firmly what the occasion called for. The gentleman only wanted to watch and would not even remove his clothes. They must, of course. The man would not touch them for a while because once he did, he came, at which point all would be over and they could leave. It never took very long. "Well,"

Fernando ordered the pair, as a foreman might his workers, "get your clothes off and get in there."

As if to demonstrate, Fernando shucked off his shirt.

Ramon and Carlos were uneasy. It was one thing to be with a man and do what he wanted: That was business. But as they did with each other what they had only been hired to do with others, it became disturbingly exciting. Each found the other's body fiery to the touch and salty to the taste. Each was achingly aware of the other. Instead of the white naked thighs of tourists straddling their chests, they saw each other's coppery bodies, and their passion became a nerve-shattering echo of masturbation before a mirror, but a mirror that touched back and kissed wetly, gripped and guided the other's erection and sighed, and sighed some more.

For his part, Mr. Tunsmith was near tears at the beauty of the scene. It was always this way for him, always this hotly intense when the boys took one another. He thought himself wise to remain clothed, to preclude their possible aversion—or his own—at his fishlike whiteness; his undulating, untamed bulk that no longer obeyed muscles and mind but was wholly subject to gravity, cascading about. Their bodies did what they bid them to do. His did what it wanted.

Although he sat directly in front of the air conditioner, Mr. Tunsmith felt parched and hot. His eyes felt scorched. He kept trying to wet his lips, but fever burned them dry.

How long had they been in the room? How much more could Mr. Tunsmith bear to watch without crying out? His erection was painfully contained in his pants, trapped between his belly and thigh. His hands were lodged between his knees, his buttocks perched on the edge of the chair. He ordered himself not to touch them yet, to stay quiet, to concentrate on controlling himself. His hands ached to fly free, and he sucked in small desperate gasps of air like a novice swimmer at the deep end of the pool. His eyes flickered over the trio as if understanding their every movement held the answers to life and death. He could weep at the thought of all these past months of passionless denial while life just ran bleakly on and out. Now that he was with his boys again he knew how dead he had felt without them, without their beauty, without the tangy spiced taste the air seemed to have when they were near and naked. For the first time in months his eyes seemed to see in the minutest detail, even in this frail light. Oh, how he wanted to slide his hand between Carlos and Ramon, to have even the most tenuous link with their passion, but he knew that if he did this the long awaited day would end.

He almost cried out when he saw Fernando straddle Ramon's head to brush his cock over Ramon's lips while Carlos sucked eagerly on Ramon's erection.

Eleven months of denial were proving too much. With frantic hands he tried to unzip his fly, but while sitting, his pants were too taut, so he stood, unzipped, grappled his cock out, and reached for Fernando, ending the afternoon in a rush.

Before the last spasm was over, Mr. Tunsmith was tottering to the bathroom, leaving Carlos and Ramon irritatedly scrubbing Mr. Tunsmith off themselves with the sheets.

Mr. Tunsmith stood well back from the door and let Fernando usher the other boys out and onto the balcony, their generous "tips" bulging in their pockets, their many parcels clutched tightly against their chests. They moved quietly toward the stairs to the central courtyard. It was remarkably still, so the shout of rage that tore through the courtyard seemed even more frightening and loud. It made the stealthy trio of boys start, and Mr. Tunsmith ran onto the balcony, expecting to find some disastrous horror. A man was screaming, "Get out! Get out!"

Derek stood on the balcony in his boxer shorts, beating on the railing and shouting at Peter, who was wrestling his large suitcase along the narrow ledge, and toward the stairs, where the three boys stood in tableau, arrested by the drama. Peter reached the stairs but couldn't get past the boys, who were not about to move along and miss the drama. Peter jabbed his suitcase at them, shouting, "Move! Goddamn it, move!"

Derek leaned over the railing to get a full view of Peter's retreat down the stairs and, seeing the boys, included them in his rage and shouted, "You're with your own kind, Peter. Now all the whores are leaving." He was readying another insult when he heard a gasp and looked up to see Mr. Tunsmith, who stood opposite. Derek shot him a look of such venomous hatred, it knocked the air out of Mr. Tunsmith.

"You get your ass back in your goddamned fucking room, fatso. This is none of your fucking business," shouted Derek as the quartet on the stairs sorted themselves out and moved down to the courtyard. When Derek turned to resume screaming at Peter, Peter was gone; only the backs of the three boys were still in sight. Derek looked up to see Mr. Tunsmith's door closed. With nowhere to hurl his bitter anger, frustration was added to Derek's rage and, goddamn it to fucking hell, he was almost out of vodka.

Ramon awoke the next morning in the tiny room he shared with two younger brothers in his mother's home. His brothers were already up and gone, giving him a rare moment of privacy in which to consider the previous day. He was still pissed off with that little fucker Carlos. What did that dumbshit think he was up to? He was ruining everything. This was only about the money.

Ramon, Carlos, and Fernando had stood opposite the hotel, watching the dark-haired man with the suitcase as he waited for his taxi. It had been too early to be hurrying back to the park, so they'd stood on the curb and conjectured over where the man was going and what the lovers had been fighting about. Would there be more drama? Would the blond follow his lover out and make an exciting scene in the street? They had waited and hoped he would.

As they'd stood giggling over one another's crudely

funny jokes about the lovers' quarrel, Carlos had kept putting his arm around Ramon and pulling him close, but it had not been like the good-natured hugs of the past—friendly, companionable hugs. No, Carlos's hugs had changed. There was more heat in the way Carlos pulled him close. Ramon was not quick, so it had taken him time to perceive what was different, but when he had he'd felt such a molten rush of sexual excitement that he ruthlessly shoved away both the feeling and Carlos. Carlos had thudded against the stucco wall and tears of pain had started down his cheeks. Ramon had seen the hurt and had wanted to pull Carlos close and comfort him; but he hadn't. That's not what men did.

The next morning Ramon woke up angry at Fernando too, because he sensed that Fernando had understood what was going on and why he had struck out at Carlos. It was all because of what happened in that fat man's room.

At the same time, just a few blocks away, Carlos awoke, sure he was in love with Ramon and not minding in the least.

But Fernando awoke more dissatisfied with his life than usual. He lay on his thin mattress on the floor, gazing at the single fly-specked lightbulb hanging from the center of the ceiling, his electronics collection—radio, Walkman, TV, CD player, watch—safely close at hand. They were all battery-powered because there was no electricity other than the light in the ceiling. There were hooks on the wall to hold his clothes and a battered plastic chair. Rooms like his were plentiful in the Zócalo, most often occupied by single men, from boys his age to men four times his seventeen years who had never moved far from Mérida's center. There they aged from the charmingly sweet male courtesans tourists coveted to working as the all but invisible shoeshine men and grifters gingerly avoided by tourists.

Even at this early hour Fernando could hear the complaining plumbing in the floor's only bathroom, which served the warren of rooms built to house 14 but housed many more. Others brought tricks and relatives here. Fernando never invited anyone to visit, much less stay. The room gave him the privacy he had longed for since childhood, when his family of eleven had denied him any solitude. Neither his few possessions nor his thoughts was ever his own. He paid a lot for this stingy slice of a once-large room, one in the maze above a seedy souvenir shop on the street below, and he thought it good value.

Fernando knew that at seventeen he was already too old for the tastes of many tourists, that his future in the park could no longer be measured in years. Then what? He knew he was smart, but that was as useless as a sixth finger in his world. He had done well at what schooling he'd been able to get for himself while living in a home repeatedly shaken by his mother's illnesses, his father's drinking, and poverty that eventually scattered the family among friends and relatives. At thirteen, Fernando had moved easily into the life of Mérida's streets, happy to find more family with his peers and customers than he ever had at home. He now had peace and regular meals, a room all his own, and a few clothes he valued and kept meticulously clean. Unlike those boys who felt used and resented those who employed them, Fernando liked love with men, and it had been so from the age of ten, from that first boy of twelve with whom he had swapped hands to masturbate.

Fernando knew his only asset was himself and that, by the standards of his trade, he had almost spent this capital. With no other asset, he knew he must find a way to capitalize on what he had left, to quickly use what abilities and opportunities lay at hand.

Derek tried not to wake up, to evade the sickening aftereffects of last night's vodka and to sink back into unconsciousness, but he couldn't. He felt faintly ill, he had the hangover hornies, he was starved, he was furious with Peter, and he wanted to kill that depraved white whale in the room opposite. That man was the kind of fat old fairy who gave gays a bad name and made them a laughingstock. Christ, the old fool had been having it off with not just one of those grubby street boys, but three? Serve him right if he caught something nasty or deadly.

Derek rolled over, not even wanting to think about what had probably gone on among them, but he did, and shuddered at the ugly images of grimy degradation that rose in his mind's eye. Those boys were victims of that fat predator. It was one thing to be gay with other gays of one's own kind and age, but it was ugly and degrading to force others to sell themselves because they were too poor to say no. And Derek was

25

sure that most of the boys he saw in the park were not gay, that they debased themselves only for money. Men like the white whale were morally contemptible and debased others to satisfy lusts that would get them arrested and despised in the States. Almost worse, the man was not only fat but also old enough to know better. Something should be done about his kind.

Concentrating on the ugly fairy opposite kept Derek from thinking that, very likely, Peter had left him for the last time. Because he sensed the finality of Peter's leaving, thinking about the white whale not only yielded a warm sense of satisfying superiority but also kept his own problems at bay.

Mr. Tunsmith sat up feeling wide awake and wonderful. He phoned in his order for a very large breakfast that was to be a feast in celebration of yesterday's beautiful afternoon, the first of many. He put on his emerald-green silk robe, opened his shutters to let in the warm light, and lay back to contemplate yesterday's excitements and anticipate today's coming adventures.

He was surprised to find he was near tears of happiness. He felt he was home and safe for the first time in almost a year. A year was a long time to feel homeless.

Mr. Tunsmith led the way from the restaurant to his hotel, with yesterday's trio of boys moving in his wake. He was still in the self-contented glow he had awakened to, and so he had gazed past the unsettling moods and atmospheres of the lunch. He hadn't noticed Fernando's long, appraising looks, missed seeing that Fernando was shaping an idea focused completely on him. He had missed Ramon's looks of confused anger at Carlos and himself, and wouldn't have cared even if he had been able to understand when Ramon said, over and over, to Carlos that he was here only for the money and to stop that fag shit. Mr. Tunsmith had noticed but took no particular interest in the frequent but tentative touches Carlos tried to give Ramon that Ramon shook off so angrily. As Mr. Tunsmith herded his troupe up the stairs he didn't see the door opposite ajar or Derek seated in the dark interior, watching them over the rim of his vodka glass.

As Mr. Tunsmith sat luxuriating in the cooled air and the sight of the beautiful Ramon slipping his shirt over his head, two policemen crashed in, and there was suddenly too much noise and light in the room. The cops shouted orders and insults at Mr. Tunsmith in Spanish and shoved him when he appeared not to know what they were ordering him to do. He stumbled about, clumsily trying to get out of their way as they marauded around the room, opening closets and drawers and throwing his clothes onto the bed and floor. They screamed abuse at the boys, who were scurrying to find their clothes and dress.

When the bedroom lay in disarray they began to ransack the bathroom, emptying the medicine cabinet and pulling things out and hurling them on the floor where they broke and were trampled, sending up a smothering miasma of heady colognes. Mr. Tunsmith covered his mouth to hold in a scream and tried to squeeze into a too-small space between the wall and an armoire.

Oh, my God, what was happening? Despite his question, he knew, and it terrified him and made him grip his behind as he felt his bowels churning.

One of the policemen furiously stamped on a plastic medicine bottle that refused to break and screamed something Mr. Tunsmith couldn't understand.

Fernando said, "They say you have drugs. Do you, Mr. Tunsmith?"

Mr. Tunsmith shook his head rapidly and felt even more afraid. Fernando said to the police, "He comes here every year. Never any drugs. Never." The police sneered but, seeing they had already had their intended effect, they grew suddenly calm. One lifted the mattress and peered under it; the other leaned against a wall.

Mr. Tunsmith shook his head as if to say there was nothing under the mattress, and Fernando said, "They may have brought drugs to plant on you."

The smaller policeman smiled slyly at Ramon and Carlos, who were again trying to get into their clothes, and told them to stop dressing, to take off the clothes they had put back on, to stay naked. They said the scene of the crime must remain as they had found it. The evidence must remain in sight so they could appraise it properly. Their sly expressions showed how pleased they were with the terrible evidence of depravity they'd uncovered: naked boys, a sweaty old Americano.

They gestured at Mr. Tunsmith to look at the
boys—the evidence against him—and the taller one
said that of course the American had the right to call
his embassy. Did the American want to call his
embassy and have them come and see for themselves?
If that was what the American wanted, they would
oblige by waiting.

Fernando translated for Mr. Tunsmith, who shook
his head but only half comprehended, still so dazed
by the suddenness of the invasion that his mind staggered far behind events.

Fernando spoke to the policemen, then said to Mr.
Tunsmith, "I've told them you're an old friend of
mine—a good man—and that you're a generous man
who rewards favors."

The taller policeman said something, and Fernando
continued, "They say they are only interested in the
morals of Mexico's young." Mr. Tunsmith could only
answer with a sickly smile and a lift of his left shoulder.
The taller policeman spoke again, and Fernando managed an almost simultaneous translation:
"They...*we*...want to do only what is best for everyone,
not cause the boys' parents more trouble than wicked
boys like these must already cause them. Terrible
things like this are best handled quietly. Is it not best
that way?" The policeman continued to speak, but
Fernando stopped translating the words and began to
suggest the solution: "I will offer them each three hundred dollars on your behalf. Can you manage that?" Mr.
Tunsmith nodded and, seeing that Fernando had
stopped speaking, the policeman stopped.

Fernando said something, the policemen consulted each other with a look, and the taller one turned to Fernando and raised five fingers. Without looking at Mr. Tunsmith, Fernando asked, "Five hundred each?"

Mr. Tunsmith looked so distraught the policemen thought they might have gone beyond his resources.

The policemen held a rapid whispered consultation and said something to Fernando, who asked, "How much can you give them? They say they'll let you keep enough to leave and get home."

Mr. Tunsmith gave them almost all his money and wept as he signed the traveler's checks that sacrificed his weeks in Mérida, and many beautiful boys, and the many lovely things he had planned to do with and for them. He signed away so much more than money, and what was painfully wrenching, he signed away an endless number of future Mérida Januarys. There would be no more.

The police said the boys could dress and leave, which they did with remarkable speed. They didn't look at Mr. Tunsmith as they raced out. Outside the hotel Ramon and Carlos ran in opposite directions and Fernando walked slowly to the Zócalo.

The policemen left after the boys, not bothering to tell Mr. Tunsmith to leave Mérida. The culprits always did, and quickly, having been left just enough to pay their hotel bill and take a cab to the airport. The policemen didn't want the hotels to suffer and, perhaps, complain and call attention to their pursuit of moral offenders, so desk clerks were rewarded for cooperating.

The policemen left Mr. Tunsmith's door ajar but not enough to afford Derek a clear look into Mr. Tunsmith's room. But Mr. Tunsmith could see him, could see the blond man peering intently from the balcony opposite, and he began to cry with shame. Mr. Tunsmith managed to get behind his door without Derek seeing him and close it. Derek felt disappointed and annoyed. It had all been so quick, barely minutes since he'd seen the police moving stealthily up the stairs. *Well,* Derek thought, *it was bound to happen to men like that, as it damned well should.*

If Mr. Tunsmith had been wearing anything but his bright white suit, Fernando might not have found him, for Mérida's small airport was thronging riotously with masses of people who had been disgorged almost simultaneously by four planes that weren't supposed to arrive all at once. The passengers milled about in confusion, losing and finding their tour directors and one another, clustering anxiously around empty luggage carousels and crowding the small dining room and bar they were quickly buying out. Spanish, German, French, and English careered through the air, sounding appeal, despair, and anger.

In the midst of these hundreds eddying about in confusion sat Mr. Tunsmith. He had almost no awareness of the hysterical scene, because he was staring through the chaos at the wounding scene in his bedroom that kept replaying itself with undiminished horror, his shame and degradation now more sharply painful because the numbness of the shock had passed. He wanted to be on his plane and away from this ugly place he had loved, half hoping that the rising plane would lift him out of this nightmare. But he sensed that this shameful afternoon would be more vividly enduring than his lovely memories of so many other beautiful Januarys. For a large part of his life he had been willing to trade eleven months of drudgery for this month, this warming month. Present shame erased future hope, and all his energy centered on not weeping here in public and debasing himself further.

Just as Fernando was sure he had missed Mr. Tunsmith, that he had arrived too late for his chance, he saw the white suit. But the white suit looked much too big on the man, and it took on a sickly greenish cast under the fluorescent lights. Mr. Tunsmith looked smaller slumped in a cheap red plastic scoop chair and staring with sad intensity into space. He knew it was Mr. Tunsmith, but how could this big, open, lively man have become so small and soiled? Fernando feared for his plan, because Mr. Tunsmith now reminded him of the old idlers who populated the Zócalo, and they were of no use to anyone, not even themselves.

Fernando planted himself in front of Mr. Tunsmith and, by habit, waited to be acknowledged, but when Mr. Tunsmith continued to stare through him, Fernando snapped, "Look up, Mr. Tunsmith. It's me."

Mr. Tunsmith looked and winced, the sight of Fernando reviving the shameful scene with more reality than he could bear. He shot to his feet and stared wild-eyed, sure the police had changed their minds and brought Fernando to the airport. He held up his hand to ward off the sight of Fernando and gave a frightened shake of his head. His whole body said *Go away!*

"You're not well, Mr. Tunsmith. Come with me. I'll get you a drink."

"No. Oh, no. You go away, Fernando. I have to leave. I just want to stay here alone. You go away. I don't have anything left."

Fernando was certainly not going away, not after he had spent so much on a cab to get here, and certainly not when he intended to turn the terrible events of this afternoon to advantage.

Fernando saw that Mr. Tunsmith didn't have the strength to resist him, so he said, "You come with me, Mr. Tunsmith. You need a drink." Mr. Tunsmith shook his head and a little shiver went through him. Fernando was exasperated and commanded, "Get up, Mr. Tunsmith, and come with me."

Mr. Tunsmith followed Fernando to the bar, dragging wearily behind the boy who was irritated by his slowness, by his acting like an old man. Fernando elbowed quickly through the crowd to a table just emptying and claimed it, waving Mr. Tunsmith over. Fernando said firmly, "Sit," and went to find a waiter. He ordered a brandy for Mr. Tunsmith and a Coke for himself.

Fernando regarded Mr. Tunsmith, who sat staring down at his hands, which lay dead in his lap. The man reminded Fernando of his sister, Isabella, when she sleepwalked. Fernando had never imagined that a time would come when he would be able to tell this rich and important man what to do, but he just had, and the man had done as he'd been told. It gave Fernando hope.

"The drink will help, Mr. Tunsmith. Drink it." Fernando pushed the glass toward him.

Mr. Tunsmith tasted the drink, realized he craved it, and drank it down in a single draught. It took away some of the chill.

Fernando nodded approval and said, "You'll have another." He got the waiter's eye and held up the empty brandy glass.

Mr. Tunsmith looked around to gauge how softly he must speak to not be overheard and asked, "How do you suppose they knew? How?"

Fernando said, "It's not important."

"How can you say that? It is important. It's all so ugly and degrading. Who could mean me harm? Who could want to hurt me so terribly? That's what scares me...knowing someone hates me enough to want to hurt me."

"It's not important. It was for money. It was not to hurt you. It is just a way to make money."

But Mr. Tunsmith couldn't leave it. "That blond man across the way was furious with me. I broke something of his. I don't even know what. I tried to pay. You saw me. Do you suppose he told? Or the desk clerk? But I was very generous with him. I hate to think it was."

"*It's not important*, Mr. Tunsmith," Fernando said irritably, shoving his Coke around the tiny table.

"It's kind of you to come to see if I'm all right. I hope what happened won't make trouble for you."

Fernando shrugged the idea aside and, feeling the

pressure of time and his own purpose, drove to his point: "Mr. Tunsmith, I want you to take me to America with you."

The idea was so surprisingly far from his own thoughts that Mr. Tunsmith wasn't sure he'd heard correctly and shook the words away with a twist of his head.

Fernando said it again: "I want you to take me to America with you, to Los Angeles. Get me a ticket and take me now."

"Oh, that's impossible. I mean I couldn't. They wouldn't let me. You have to have papers or something."

"Then arrange it for me, Mr. Tunsmith."

"Oh, I couldn't."

"A lawyer could. I can work. My English is good. I'm smart. Take me."

"They wouldn't let me. The police."

"Then send for me."

"I couldn't."

"You have a lover in America?"

"No."

"You live alone?"

"Yes."

"Good. You live alone. You have no lover. I live alone. No one misses me. I go to America and no one even notices I've left."

Mr. Tunsmith understood that.

"If you can't take me now, send for me. There's nothing more for me here. I will be good for you."

Mr. Tunsmith didn't know what to say. He looked

sadly at Fernando and thought, *He does look so much older. He's not a boy this year. He was last year. He was so sweet, and only just last year. But he'll soon be a man and start showing the years, even at twenty.*

Then, without seeing any irony, he thought, *I suppose he can't help getting older. I couldn't.* He looked at Fernando and wanted to do something for him.

He asked, "Will the police give you more trouble, Fernando? Tell me. That would be terrible. If you want to leave Mérida, I could send you money when I get home. I have barely enough. They took it all." He stopped speaking and looked as if he were about to cry.

Fernando knew the police wouldn't bother him now that they had their money, but it seemed worth letting Mr. Tunsmith think they would: "Yes, it will be difficult for me now. They will keep after me. That is why I am asking you to help me."

"I'll send you money. You know I will."

"I want to go to America with you, stay with you."

"It's complicated and I can't think now."

He had to think now. Fernando pressed on: "It can be done."

It was now or never. Mr. Tunsmith would never be here again, never be more likely to say yes than he was now. The commitment had to be now.

"If you can't take me, send for me. If you're alone, there's room for me, isn't there?"

"There's no one at the house."

"Give me your address and phone number. Tell me how to get in touch with you. There's no way you can call me."

Mr. Tunsmith began rummaging in his pockets for a piece of paper and finally tore off a corner of his boarding envelope and began writing. He handed Fernando the paper and Fernando held it tightly, feeling that he held his first piece of life in America. He had somewhere to go, and someone would be there to take him in. If he went he could not be lost, would not be alone or hungry. He held an IOU for a future and he could have wept with gratitude but knew that would not be right, that Mr. Tunsmith would not like being embarrassed in public.

"You will be happy to have me there, Mr. Tunsmith. You can depend on me and I can be useful."

"Oh, I wouldn't bring you there to put you to work."

"I want to work. I'm getting older. I should learn to do something. I can make things better for you."

"You don't have to, Fernando."

"Why not? Why shouldn't I? I'm not a child."

A speaker cawed an announcement.

"My plane," said Mr. Tunsmith.

He started to rise, and Fernando laid a hand on his arm.

"You promise, Mr. Tunsmith. Please promise. I know I can trust you."

It made no sense, but Mr. Tunsmith promised.

Mr. Tunsmith spent most of the flight thinking that what Fernando had proposed was out of the question, impossible, probably expensive and tricky, and something he would very likely do, would try very hard to do, because his flight was taking him home to nothing.

He reopened his shop as soon as he got home.

For years there had been nothing Mr. Tunsmith had truly wanted; working to get Fernando to America gave him purpose, something that took energy he hadn't needed in years. He felt a sense of purpose he'd forgotten.

When there was an actual date for Fernando's arrival, there was the house to get ready, Fernando's room to be decorated. Fernando must have his own room. Mr. Tunsmith didn't want it to look...well, to look like he expected Fernando to share his bed. But he longed, he dreamed.

Fernando proved to be intelligent and energetic, bossy and overbearing, shrewd about money, and shrewish about Mr. Tunsmith's lazy business habits and foolish eating. "Who wants to sleep with a cow?" he'd yell when he caught Mr. Tunsmith at the Oreos or Milk Duds, and he would snatch them away and storm off to dispose of them. The ladies who came to the shop loved Fernando and thought the noticeably trimmer Mr. Tunsmith lucky to have such a good, sensible boy in his life. Mr. Tunsmith grumbled about being bossed, but it suited him and made him feel as if he were important to Fernando. All Mr. Tunsmith fretted about was how quickly Fernando learned. After all, if Fernando learned enough, might he not become independent and leave? But Fernando stayed.

Fernando was happy. He quickly learned that in America good things must be replaced by better things as quickly as possible, and he set about improving their lives. He knew he made life better for Mr.

Tunsmith and made him happy. Little by little Mr. Tunsmith forgot that dreadful business in Mérida. As Fernando said, "What did that afternoon with the police matter? Isn't life better for both of us? Forget it." So, like most of what Fernando ordered him to do, Mr. Tunsmith did. As for himself, Fernando remembered that day with gratitude.

It pleased Fernando to think that all that foolish Ramon had gotten from the police was a meager kickback, while he, Fernando, had been given a future.

LUST'S LABORS LOST

3:45 P.M.

He answered his office phone with a hard "Yes!" meant to convey that he was an overly busy man up to his ears in work, that he could permit no long pointless chat, and that the caller was to present his case with dispatch and not linger.

The caller said, "Bernie, it's Frank." Bernie's heart rate sped up. "Look, Bernie, I know this is short notice, but I'm filling in for a friend on the four o'clock out of Atlanta and I'm going to have about three hours in New York before I have to fly back. I hoped I could see you."

Bernie's concentration flew from his office to Atlanta. *Oh, God yes, Frank. Fly north, come to me, ravish me, bring turmoil to my bed and lust to my loins.*

Bernie's tongue was fixed to the roof of his mouth, and he tried to not sound like an addict offered a fix when he answered, "Hey, sure. It would be nice to see you again." Sensing that cool might have edged into chilly, he added, "I've really missed seeing you."

"Terrific! I figure I can be at your place about seven. I'll have to be on my way by nine, but that gives us two hours. I'm glad I got a hold of you. It's been a long time. Gotta run. See you in a few."

Bernie hung up with a care that suggested the phone was made of crystal. His headlong day had suddenly ground into slow motion, his pressing deadline almost forgotten. After ten months, Frank was returning. The best sex he had ever had was flying to New York and in about three hours would be at his door and moments later (if there was a God) would be in his bed.

Ten months ago Frank's airline had changed his route and their months of startling, mind-melting sex had ended, and Bernie had wept, not for the loss of love or illusion but for what seemed to him the loss of his entire body, of the sixth—even seventh—sense Frank had endowed him with. Frank had awakened his whole being. The ends of his fingers had seemed to vibrate when he touched Frank, every hair on his body had felt separate and responsive, his tongue had felt more natural in Frank's mouth than in his own, and there had been times when he felt that even his fingernails possessed nerve endings. Then came Frank's devastating transfer that was like a sentence to sensual mediocrity. Without Frank to feel him, to curl over and around him, to caress him, Bernie seemed to have lost large areas of his body. Colors were shades dimmer, sounds dulled, other bodies were not as smooth or warm or real. He had experienced the past few months like a patient consigned to tranquilized carnality.

At least that's how it had seemed until Dan. Dan had...

Oh, my God, he had a date with Dan. And Dan was sweet and beautiful and endearing. Dan was wonderful fun and Bernie could see a future with him. Dan was so much he wanted.

Dan wasn't Frank.

His secretary shook him out of his reverie by bolting into his office out of breath, dumping a tall pile of paper on the corner of his desk, and gasping, "Typing is ready for the next batch and graphics is almost done with the first ten charts."

It took him a long moment to fight his way out of his trance and remember who this distraught woman was. She looked like she'd just finished an aerobics class. But Miss McGuane always disintegrated as the day went on, illustrating how hard she worked.

He said, "Good, Norah," being not quite sure just what was "good." Oh, yes, the toothpaste account his agency was bidding on. But now the product that had been the focus of his whole world for the past month seemed suddenly mundane, even pointless. He tried to shift his focus from Frank to toothpaste and said, "I'll have the next pages ready to go in a few minutes. Why don't you go down to the cafeteria and take a break?"

She seemed confused by his unusual proposal of rest in the midst of an exhilarating crisis, but smiled and said, "I won't be gone for more than five minutes."

"Make it ten," he said, and she left reluctantly.

He refocused to find himself surrounded by the mass of paper that dealt with demographics and target markets, color research and the viscosity of paste, of tubes versus pumps. It all seemed suddenly and immensely irrelevant. The presentation to the client was tomorrow morning at ten. The typing and graphics people were standing by to labor through the night, if necessary. He had planned to stay to marshal these forces, refine and remake the work. This job was *important*, millions in potential billings at stake. But come hell or high water, he would be out of this joint by five. Frank was coming.

He attacked the stacks of paper, sorting, renumbering pages, correcting graphs, selecting slides, and hoping he knew what the hell he was doing. But he was sure he worked better under pressure. It sharpened him, made him quick and acute. He certainly hoped it did.

Miss McGuane returned and stood by, quivering with energy, ready to dart off with pages and drawings as Bernie handed them to her. He tried to look the model of decisiveness in the face of rising panic, praying the thought of Frank wasn't scrambling his skill and precision.

As he worked at double time, other thoughts kept intruding, and he noted them on a pad while pressing into the paperwork.

4:50 P.M.

Miss McGuane stood with the last of the job clutched to her bosom, ready to charge off.

"I've got to get out of here, Norah. I have a major emergency. So I probably won't be here when you get back from typing. But tell that sonuvabitch Boyce that if this job isn't bound and ready for me at eight tomorrow morning I'll have his ass."

She smiled as bravely as a heroine about to leave on a suicide mission, eager to be off to threaten that sonuvabitch Boyce.

Her "Yes, sir!" held all her determination and bravery, and she spun around and was gone, leaving Bernie to give his notes a quick review. They read:

Sheets

Champagne

Shower

Where put Boo?

Postpone Dan!?

His list had to be completed in less than two hours. Could it? It must be.

He dialed Lou. "Lou, love. Big favor. The hot water in my building is off. Can I come by and take a shower? I'll even bring my own towels."

"Sure, but why would you have to bring towels?"

"Don't want to inconvenience you. And could you do me a really big favor and keep Boo for a couple of hours?"

"Shower, yes. Boo, no. Boo hates me. He starts howling the minute you're out the door, and when he's not howling he's pissing on everything."

"I know he can be a bit of trouble, but it's terribly important. Do you think I'd ask if it wasn't an emergency?"

"What emergency?"

"It's private."

"You mean it's a secret?"

"It's not a secret. I just can't tell you."

And he couldn't. Lou was one of Dan's best friends. Lou was one of his best too, but Lou could be a prude.

"I'll take you to dinner, Lou. Whatever restaurant, no matter how expensive."

"It's that Frank, isn't it?"

Panic. "What Frank?"

"Flying Frank. That Olympic-class fuck of yours. That's 'what Frank.' He fall out of the sky again?"

"No. It's something else."

"I suppose I'm not supposed to say anything to Dan about what's going on."

Lou had him.

"Can I bring Boo over when I come to shower?"

"Only if he leaves with you."

"Sure," Bernie said in a bereaved tone he hoped made Lou feel guilty, and hung up.

Some friend! Well, as long as he didn't tell Dan.

Now, Dan. What could he tell him? The best thing was not to plan his excuse in advance. Bernie always lied most effectively when he improvised. He dialed and was relieved when Dan's machine answered the phone: "Dan, it's Bernie. You're going to hate me, but I've gotten way behind on this toothpaste presentation and I have to stay. I wish I knew how long, but I don't. I'll try you again later."

He glanced up to be sure Miss McGuane wasn't near, then said to Dan's machine, "I love you and I hate like hell not to be able to see you tonight."

5:15 P.M.

His subway train sat in the tunnel while tinny speakers chewed up an announcement. Bernie fumed, thinking that if Paul Revere had to take the damned subway we'd still be a British colony.

The train lurched forward and his heart leapt. Then it jerked again and stopped, leaving him near tears. He had to get to Macy's and buy sheets. Safe sex might save lives, but it was sure hell on the laundry. And last night with Dan and the new videotapes had left his bed a battlefield.

Bernie didn't want his reunion with Frank to be on anything but pristine sheets, the best sheets Macy's had to offer, sheets of surpassing smoothness and luxury.

The train lurched and moved, and kept moving.

Oh, God, he didn't have his Macy's charge card with him and he was maxed on the others. Not enough left to make a dash to a cash machine worthwhile. Well, he'd just have to pay cash, which meant it would have to be California champagne. By the time he bought the champagne, he'd have barely enough left for bus fare.

5:57 P.M.

He tugged the sheets off the bed and cursed Boo, who thought changing sheets was a great game and kept leaping and prancing on the bed as Bernie snarled at him. Finally, he had to lock Boo in the bathroom, where he howled and clawed at the door. Boo was a peculiar presence in Bernie's life. What had started as an enchanting puppy had grown into a large, furry, rather alarming mammal of puzzling origins.

He tugged the sheets smooth, slipped into shorts and a T-shirt, leashed Boo, and headed toward the door with the haste of someone fleeing a burning building.

Lou just had to keep Boo. Boo resented it when Bernie closed his bedroom door and would fling ninety-two pounds of mongrel resentment against the offending door and outraged noises that weren't at all doglike and that made Bernie think of Wolfman movies. Boo's assaults scattered his concentration, and despite his assurances to his trick that Boo was just curious, the trick's attention usually shifted from passion to panic.

Bernie considered the bribes likely to make Lou abandon his scruples about Boo: a silk shirt, a Broadway show, a superb dinner. He considered several lavish possibilities as he hurried down West Twenty-third Street toward Lou's. Lou could have anything. Frank was worth anything.

6:15 P.M.

Lou watched and considered as Bernie hastily dried himself. It had to be that Frank or some new number. Either way he was being asked to abet the betrayal of Dan. Bernie used to ask his upstairs neighbor to take Boo when he had some number by, but the neighbor had moved.

Well, he certainly wasn't going to double-cross his good friend Dan just so Bernie could screw around. Not even if Bernie offered him a shopping spree. Not even that very expensive shirt he'd seen at Barneys would be enough to buy betrayal. Almost, but not quite. Even the Bronx Zoo would draw the line at Boo.

Bernie was dressed and he slipped his watch on, noting that it read 6:35. Bernie made one last try: "*Two* of those shirts you want at Barneys." He saw Lou waver and was relieved to see that Lou was beginning to look shifty. Just as Bernie was sure he'd bagged him, Lou's doorbell rang and he went to the intercom to buzz Dan in.

He turned to Bernie and said, "It's Dan."

Bernie looked stricken, and Lou said, "I wasn't expecting him."

"Then why?"

"Returning some tapes I loaned him, I suppose. I take it from your expression that you don't want him to see you."

Bernie felt too abashed to answer.

"You want to hide?"

Bernie looked uncertain.

"I wouldn't hide you for your sake, Bernie. You're acting like a shit. It's for Dan's sake. I don't want him hurt."

"Where?"

"There's only the bedroom," Lou said, then went to answer Dan's knock.

Bernie wavered, then tugged the resisting Boo into the bedroom and pulled the door closed. He heard Lou open the door and remembered that Boo always yelped and pranced at the sound of Dan's voice. Bernie heard Dan say "Hi, Lou," and Boo began to caper and bay.

Bernie opened the door to see a startled Dan and a sour Lou staring at him. Improvisation failed him. All he could think of were excuses that were so surpassingly stupid he dismissed them all.

Dan said, "Your message said..."

Bernie suppressed a mad urge to curtsy and settled for bowing his neck in a gesture that might have been either submission or anticipation of the snick of the guillotine.

They stood in frozen tableau. Bernie said, "I'm sorry." Lou said, "I'll explain," and Dan said, "Don't."

Bernie shook off Boo, who had begun to hump his right leg, and the abrupt action popped out his left contact lens. He fled without it.

6:55 P.M.

He was sure he knew what Judas felt like as he tethered Boo to the tree in front of his building. He kept assuring Boo that this wouldn't be for long, that liver or a steak would be his reward if he didn't uproot the tree and if he wouldn't hate him. He backed away from Boo, who looked curious, then suspicious, then injured and angry as Bernie backed up the stairs toward the front door. He swept through the door as Boo let out a howl of rage that would have stopped a rampaging elephant.

Bernie almost wept with frustration and regret as he bounded up the stairs, thankful that his apartment was at the rear of the building, where Boo's protests would only reach faintly, like some distant mob violence.

There wouldn't be time to straighten out the sordid mess into which the apartment had fallen during the past busy weeks, so he just wouldn't turn on the lights in the living room and would just heave the worst of the mess into closets.

7:01 P.M.

The last pile of magazines and laundry shot into the closet as his doorbell rang. His heart stopped, his breath grew shallow, and he sped toward his door and flung it open to see his neighbor from across the hall.

"Mrs. Millstein?"

When she saw Bernie she clasped her hands to her bosom and shut her eyes, saying, "Thank God! I was sure it was burglars. I was sure the criminals lured your dog into the street with steak and left him there so they could take their time robbing your apartment. Whoosh! Just like that, they're down the stairs with your new television and your stereo and your mother's good silver. Whoosh! So what is it?"

The downstairs bell rang and, without asking who it was, Bernie buzzed his visitor in.

"And that's how we get robbed in this building," she said. "You don't ask who, you buzz the evildoer in, and the rapist's at your door saying he's delivering flowers. Some flowers. And no Boo to defend you. So why's your dog down there waking the dead?"

The eagerly smiling Frank rounded the turn in the stairs. Mrs. Millstein glanced knowingly from one to the other and exhaled a knowing "ohhh" that conveyed complete understanding and complete disapproval, and bustled back to her apartment, her mules slapping, her tongue clicking out *Tch, tch, tch!*

8:15 P.M.

Bernie walked Frank downstairs. Boo sneezed when he saw Bernie, then whimpered, making Bernie feel even worse. Well, Boo could have the ground sirloin he'd planned to cook for himself for dinner. He wasn't hungry.

He had planned a longer farewell to Frank, but Frank was fidgeting, obviously anxious to be away.

"Yeah, well, good to see you, Bernie. Gotta run."

"Sure."

Bernie was still untying Boo when he saw Frank climb into a cab down at the corner.

10:05 P.M.

A large straight gin and a large joint hadn't taken the edge off.

He'd probably fucked up some of the toothpaste material, Boo was ignoring him, Lou probably thought him a devious fool, Mrs. Millstein would purse her lips and "tch!" at him for weeks, and Dan wasn't the kind to shrug off such a hurtful and stupid deception. He'd even spent all his cash on sheets and would have to grub car fare from whatever change he could find in drawers and pockets to get to work.

And for what?

Indeed, for what? Frank looked the same...trim, lively, enchanting, exciting. So why? Where had the magic gone? Frank once made his ears ring and his toes curl, his knees quiver, and his eyes feel feverish. Frank had lost his silkiness, he was several degrees cooler to the touch, and seemed to have developed a squint. And worst of all, Frank's saliva had grown gooey. Where had the magic fled? When had the caviar turned into unborn fish?

He looked sadly toward Boo, who stood and stared at him.

Well, Boo, he thought, *even after all I've done to you tonight, you're still with me, you still love me.* He made kissing noises and looked fondly at Boo as he held out his beckoning hands.

Boo turned away and raised his hind leg at the sofa.

STEALING BACK

Imagine you've fallen off a cliff and you're halfway to the jagged rocks below when, magically, you're slowly floating back to the cliff's edge where you started. You were that close to dead and now you're not. That might be commonplace in dreams, but in real life it's disorienting, and all you can do is wonder, *Good sweet Jesus, what's happening? What now? What next?*

It's more than likely that I'm going to live.

You'd think I'd be dancing in the street and wanting to tell everyone the good news. But it feels too unreal—something like a lie—so full of uncertainty that I can't bring myself to say it aloud.

Another reason I'm quiet is that I don't want to hear what my friends might have to say. I'm afraid they'll say "Isn't that great news?" and I'll think, *I don't know.* Or they'll say "Isn't that exciting?" and I'll think *So's tightrope-walking blindfolded.* How do you tell people that you're confused or reluctant, even unhappy, about getting well?

So far I've gained about ten pounds and my face doesn't look so whittled down. I look in my mirror and no longer see a sack of bones a dog would turn up his nose at. I'm two months along with what they call the "cocktail," an odd name for a witch's brew of medicines that run my day.

I'm even getting semi–self-sufficient, but I'm wary. It took so much work, time, tears, and fury to put together the ramshackle machine that's kept me going that I'm afraid to even think about taking it apart. What if I have a setback and have to go back to square one? Getting food stamps, Medicaid, home help—all that's kept me going—was a unique kind of hell.

Take the welfare people. They insist that you get down to basics.

I have a rented apartment that's pretty small for what I pay, but the place seemed to get bigger as I gave away what I couldn't sell. As I shrank I gave clothes away. After I'd had one too many accidents on the sofa, Jimmy came by with a friend and hauled it down four flights to the street and dumped it on the curb. The rug went after I slipped on it and fell a couple of times. I'm down to my bed, a couple of side tables, and a battered armchair an ugly shade of brown that always makes me think of a hunchbacked teddy bear. There's a TV and VCR, a couple of vinyl kitchen chairs, and the drop leaf table. One of the side tables is just for medications. It looks like a yellow chess set with way too many pieces.

Before welfare kicked in, I was pretty desperate for money and too proud to ask for help, so Louis sold my few treasures on eBay. These were things I'd loved and rescued from my mother's yard sales. I sold my eight GI Joes and fifteen copies of early X-Men comics. I should be too old to miss things like that, but it hurt like hell to part with them.

I've become like those people you see on the evening news fleeing invading armies. They're slogging along muddy roads with their whole lives loaded into a wheelbarrow or a baby carriage. I used to wonder what they hauled along; now I have a pretty good idea. Oddly, I like knowing how little I need.

Not numbered among my declarable assets was a lover, but he couldn't take what was happening to me and ran...all the way to San Francisco. He couldn't take seeing all the juice run out of me, or all those evenings with nothing but television and me sobbing willy-nilly over the damnedest things...*The Simpsons*, the evening news, dog food commercials. He couldn't stand knowing the bars were full of healthy possibilities. Worst of all, he couldn't take having to buy me Depends.

By the time he pulled out, it was something of a relief. When he was around a Sondheim lyric ran through my head; something about "martyred looks, cryptic sighs / Sullen glares from those injured eyes."

One day I went to one of my dozen or so doctors, and when I got home he was gone. He took my suitcase, but I wasn't going anywhere. At least he had the grace to not leave a note, so I was spared any of the regretful bullshit he might have thought I'd eat.

It's almost sad to think that when I first laid eyes on him, all I wanted to do was fall on my knees and claw at his zipper. It's sadder to think that he left nothing, not even empty space or a sense of loss.

So, now that I'm down to the bare essentials, it seems that some kind of life may be necessary.

I've been sneaking out on my own. I'm tottery, but I'm not leaning on someone.

The first time I went out it was daytime, but I was afraid someone would see me and learn my secret, so I've taken to going out after I take my three A.M. pills. Not that time has any meaning after all these months. When you're housebound for so long, whether it's high noon or high night is meaningless. Time is for people with schedules, places to go.

Night is also better because that first walk scared the hell out of me. Cars seemed to be going at least ninety. Everybody was racing along, even old ladies on walkers. The noise, the horns, kids slicing between people on skateboards, women using baby strollers like battering rams, crazed delivery people riding bicycles on the sidewalk, all of them some new peril I could barely remember.

I've made it all the way down four flights and around the block a few times. Last week I even made it to the all-night supermarket—three whole blocks. I wasn't up to carrying anything home, but it was suddenly a possibility. Now I think about going back and buying stuff I probably shouldn't eat, even standing in one of those lines I used to hate. I entertain myself by making lists of foods that are probably bad for me: Twinkies and Cheetos, beer nuts, and that gelatinous Chef Boyardee spaghetti I love.

Night people are different from the day ones and not as unnerving. They're fewer and more distinct. I sometimes sit on the steps of the church around the corner and watch them. I imagine that the fast ones are getting off work and going home and that the slow ones are on their way to work. The rubbery drunks don't seem to know where they're going. And it's fascinating to look down five or six long blocks and see only a car or two.

One lovely thing about being out at night is walking past Santelli's bakery at around four in the morning when they load the air with yeast and sugar and vanilla. For the first time in ages, my mouth waters and I feel real hunger. I've eaten all kinds of guaranteed-healthy stuff for so long, hunger pangs are a poignant surprise.

My caregiver still comes, and I certainly wouldn't mind seeing the last of Don. We don't like each other, never have. I've no idea why neither of us asked for a change. We could have.

For my part, it was probably perversity.

While I was sinking from sight, I felt less and less, but what I got from Don was a real feeling. It was a feeling of annoyance, but it was something; it stirred me up when little else did.

Don is bossy and fussy and exudes the plastic cheer of a garden gnome. His permanent smile looks like it was painted on by a clumsy embalmer.

It may be hard to believe, but at the start of my end I actually liked what was happening. It was great to not have to get up and go to the technical writing job I loathed. The job paid well, I was good at it, and it was numbingly dull. But I'd majored in English, and that almost left me equipped to manage a McDonald's. I was also glad not to have to go up and down four flights that grew steeper and more perilous every day. Best of all, I was relieved to have a reason to stop going to memorial services for my friends.

Now that I was going to be home every day I thought I could finally spend time on my own writing, what I thought of as "real writing." It was all I'd thought about for years. I'd have time. But now I couldn't remember one thing I'd once ached to say or one great writer I'd once longed to emulate. I'd become a blank page.

While dying is a fairly big problem, it also solves a lot of little ones. You stop worrying about whether what you wear is hot, and which gym and what bars are in, and whether you'll find a lover or whether you'll lose a lover or why the lover you're stuck with won't go away.

I settled into being looked after and tried not to resent what can feel more like charity than friendship. (Is it stating the obvious to say that I also resented their good health and that they could take for granted things I longed to do?) People brought me videos, newspapers, books, gossip, and healthy foods a rabbit would snub. For reasons I hope I never understand, my mother sent me a subscription to a horoscope magazine and a Tibetan prayer wheel. My sister sends me clippings from checkout tabloids about arcane medical theories and bizarre cures.

People bring me restorative herbs that smell as if they've been gathered under a full moon in an abandoned graveyard. They bring me theories: The dreaded "it" isn't caused by HIV; a CIA lab accidentally released AIDS; Nostradamus said this would happen; the whole mess started when some guy ate a badly cooked monkey.

Every goddamned one of them meant well, but people's ideas of being helpful and supportive can take curious turns. Fred brought me the Hemlock Society's book, *Let Me Die Before I Wake*, about what they call "self-deliverance"—i.e., suicide. I couldn't tell if he meant it as solace or suggestion.

Even worse, Larry brought me that Kübler-Ross book on the five stages of dying. I read some of it. I read enough to learn that dying people are supposed to die in stages, like tourists with a strict itinerary. But what if I got my dying out of order—would I get a failing grade? What if I did the last "stage" first and the first last? Among the stages she enumerated, "pissed off" wasn't among them. She may have been snooping on the dying, but wait till she got around to doing it. Take it from me, there's no orderly march to the grave. It's more like a drunk dancing on a suspension bridge. But then there are practical friends like Sam, who pays my cable bill, and Nick, who pays for my phone and electric. Best of all, there's Bea and Chris who make me laugh till tears and snot run down my face.

I try to think of things that would lure me back into the world. There's the idea of movies on big screens with deafening sound tracks, rather than epics all scrunched onto a seventeen-inch TV set. I'd like to wander around Barnes & Noble for hours. I'd find sidewalk cafes and sit for hours watching beautiful men. But I'd just watch, because even thinking about sex scares the hell out of me.

And then there are the things that make me want to keep hiding out. Every so often I work up the guts to look at the want ads in the paper, but I come across words like "fast-paced" and "challenging" and feel exhausted. There've been days when it's taken me fifteen minutes to make a peanut butter–and–jelly sandwich.

Could I go back to squandering time on lifeless work? And what about my skills? Would they come back, or would I face a computer with no idea how to make it work? Am I out-of-date?

I sometimes stand in my window and watch people hurrying around and try to remember what used to be important enough to get me out there. What drove me? What did I think was so urgent?

I'm leery of inching back—returning all the way—even most of the way. I'm not sure I have the courage, because someday I'll have to start dying all over again.

I suppose I'll have to come back. But who will I be? What have I become? Where will I fit?

I'm pretty sure I've become someone else; I just don't know who he is.

LEAST SAID

She dialed the long-distance number wrong, then slammed the receiver down, angry at the unfamiliar voice that answered. She gulped a sharp, exasperated breath and dialed again, and again heard the wrong voice. Angry tears came, so she put the receiver down delicately and sat back, forcing her tense hands into her lap, working to counterfeit calm. She breathed deeply and ordered her feelings to behave, but her mind raced with dreadful messages.

When she could, she dialed again, and this time the phone rang on and on. That was good. For some reason she was comforted by the ringing, by a sound she usually hated. The mechanically orderly trill now seemed a sign of normalcy in a disordered world. She knew her sister's schedule and felt sure that she must be home alone at ten in the morning. She had chosen this hour carefully. Cory and Debbie would be in school, Henry at his insurance company, the breakfast mess cleared, beds...

"Hello," she heard her sister Grace say breathlessly.

"Did I catch you at a bad time?" Claire asked.

"Out in the garden, fiddling with that damned lawn mower. It's acting up again. Been ringing long?"

"Huh?"

Grace imagined Claire sitting on the hallway stairs next to the phone table. Claire's knees would be drawn near her chin and she would be looking distractedly at her nail polish for flaws. "Huh?" was Claire's call for attention, her signal to her older sister that she must meet some need, solve some problem. "Huh?" made Grace responsible for searching out Claire's pain *and* for prescribing the cure.

Grace asked the question their mother always had: "What's the matter, dear?"

"This is really awful. So awful. I don't even know how to talk about it."

"It's not about Gary?"

"Gary's fine. No, he's not. I mean, there's no problem between us, and he's not sick or anything."

"Has the doctor told you something?"

"Thank God, no. Oh, no."

"The children?"

"Well, Dukey and Chrissy are fine..."

"Not Kevin?" Grace asked, feeling an alarm she tried to keep out of her voice. The boy was her favorite. He was the first of her sister's three children, the first grandchild in the family, with her own first, Cory, coming three months later.

"What about Kevin, dear? Just take your time and tell me."

Grace knew her sister well enough to know she

needed time to put her troubles into words, but it could be irritating. With Claire the problem might be a shade larger than nothing or a disaster. Grace pressed her impatience down.

When she could no longer stand the silence, Grace asked "Can I help?" and immediately knew she'd been drawn once again into volunteering.

"Oh, dear God, I wish you could. It's so terrible. All I can think of is those dreadful stories that are always on the news about some stranger who walks into some perfectly lovely house and murders every-body...some horror that just comes out of nowhere and gets dropped on you, ruins your life forever." Claire stopped and began to sob in stuttering gasps.

"What's the matter with Kevin? You know I'll do anything I can. Please, Claire, what's going on?"

Claire said softly, "Kevin was molested," as if she believed the words too heavy and terrible to be borne over the frail wire that connected them.

"Oh! When? Who did it?"

"Two days ago. Who knows who did it? Some man. After school. In a car. And he comes home and just tells me, blurts it right out. Just like that, he walks into the kitchen and tells me and asks me why the man did those...I don't know what horrible things."

Now that Claire was started, Grace knew the story would come in a disorderly tumble that she would have to put in order. Grace pictured her sister's dart-ing eyes, her sister's hands jabbing through her hair.

"On Monday, after school. If I've told him once... And this man comes over to Kevin and Kevin just goes with him to God knows where. That boy knows better. I've taught him better. Then he comes into the kitchen and dumps this awful... And I was already late with dinner. And you know what? I don't think he even knew it was wrong. He just spills it out, and I wanted to be sick. Just like that he says it, like asking for ice cream money. How could he? Eight years old and—"

"Was Kevin hurt?"

"What?"

"Was he hurt?"

"What kind of question is that? He was manhandled by some pervert."

"I mean, how...how far did the man go?"

"What?" Claire asked and then understood. "How could you even think such a thing, much less ask? You don't really think I'd go into details about this kind of thing? That's why we didn't call the police. It's awful enough without having to go into ugly details, have police cars pulling up in front of the house, have the neighbors gawking, asking questions."

Change tack, Grace thought. "How's Gary handling this?"

"You know Gary. Who knows? Of course he's upset. He's not a man who talks about his feelings, but they're there. He's like your Henry. And what could Gary say? His own son involved in something like this? But I know it's tearing him apart. I certainly know what it's doing to me."

"Has Gary talked to Kevin?"

"Dear sweet Jesus, what could he say?"

"I don't want to upset you, Claire. I'm not asking any of this out of idle curiosity."

"I know," she said and sighed with exhaustion.

"Can I ask something?"

"Sure."

"You won't be upset?"

"No more than I am."

"What about a therapist?"

"Nobody's crazy, just damned upset."

"I meant for Kevin."

"This is a family problem. We can handle it in the family," Claire said with an ironclad finality that Grace knew ended further discussion.

"What about Pastor Whatsisname?"

"Warner. Pastor Warner. And what could he do?"

"But what about Kevin?"

"Oh, he seemed to take it just fine. Walks in the kitchen and spews it out, calm as you please."

Grace understood. Claire had seized her problem as she had her toys, hugging it and resisting all efforts to share it, crying, "Mine! Mine!" So Grace knew what her next question must be, what Claire expected to hear, and what Grace knew she would offer for Kevin, even if it meant disrupting her own life. Grace asked, "What can I do to help?"

Claire's answer came with astonishing speed: "Take him."

"What?"

"I mean, take Kevin for a while until we can sort this out and calm down. It's impossible to get a grip on this with him around."

"You mean with Kevin around?"

"Dukey and Chrissy don't know what's going on, just that something is very wrong. What can you tell children that young? I'm keeping Kevin in his room."

"Claire, you're losing me. Is Kevin ill? Did this man hurt him?"

"I told you no."

"Then why keep him—"

"He's had an ordeal."

"What do Chrissy and Dukey think is the matter?"

"I told them I'm afraid he's coming down with something catching and I don't want to take a chance on them getting it. That's what I told them at school."

"But isn't Kevin—"

"I'm not sending him to school, having him blabbing. You sound as if you'd know just how to handle this if you were here. You're so smart, you want to come here and do that? I'll be happy to pack a bag and go someplace, anyplace."

"You know I don't butt in where I'm not wanted. I just want to help."

"I know, I know. It's just that everything is sky-high. This mess on top of everything else. Gary may get another promotion, and that could mean our third move in eight years. Another transfer and another house and a new orthodontist and different schools and more people I've never laid eyes on, and just when the garden..." She began to cry.

"There, there, dear," Grace cooed. "Of course I'll take Kevin. But it's the middle of the school year. What will I tell... Well, I'll just think of something to tell the children. I'll work it out with Henry. Leave it to me. When?"

"Soon. Two days? That give you enough time?" Claire said with such swift sureness that Grace felt irritated. Claire had probably already booked a flight for the boy. That would be like Claire, to ask for advice and help when she already knew exactly what answers she could pry out. *Well,* Grace thought, *I should be used to her by now.*

Grace said, "Then why don't we say two days. You coming with him?"

"Oh, no," Claire said. "I'll see him onto the plane and let you know when you can pick him up."

"Sure."

Grace knew better than to ask for how long, so asked, "What about school?"

"He'll just have to catch up or lose a grade. If we have to move again, it won't make much difference."

"Can I talk to him?"

"He's in his room."

Grace knew that meant no. Grace risked a question: "You haven't said how Kevin is taking all this. I mean, is he badly upset?"

"Don't you think he should be? You ask me, he's not nearly upset enough. He certainly knew better."

"Oh, Claire, he's only eight, just a baby."

When Grace's husband got home she took him up to their bedroom and the children rolled their eyes, knowing it meant trouble or money. Cory asked his sister, "You do something?"

She shook her head. "You?"

He shrugged and said, "Who knows?"

Upstairs, Grace finished her story while Henry stared at a door.

"And what are we supposed to do with him?" Henry asked.

"Just keep him awhile."

"How long?"

"Who knows?"

"We supposed to get him some kind of help here? What?"

"We're just going to...well, just baby-sit. I know better than to do anything. Claire would have my head if I interfered."

"What's he supposed to do all day while the kids are in school?"

"I'll work it out."

"Why should we have to?"

"You know Claire."

"If she can't cope, why should you?"

"Because I'm the family coper, and I love Kevin."

"And what about our kids?"

"What about them?"

"I mean, what did Kevin do with this guy?"

"Nothing."

"All this is about nothing?"

In the car on the back road, the man's hands had traveled over Kevin so lightly that the child laughed, thinking it was like the tickling game his father used to play with him. The man held Kevin's face to his chest and fondled him, kissed the top of the boy's head, and said, over and over, "Such a good boy. Such a sweet boy," until the man's breath came in spasms that slowed and ended in a sigh.

When the car pulled back on the main road, the man said, "Now you must be a good boy and not tell anybody about our game."

"Why?" Kevin asked.

"Because it's our secret. You know what a secret is. Secrets are sacred. Don't you ever keep secrets?"

Kevin looked serious as he thought about this. He tried to think of any secrets he had and couldn't. He sometimes said bad words he heard but never near home or teachers. But this didn't feel like much of a secret. Secrets were supposed to be exciting and, as the man had touched him, Kevin had felt that it wasn't much fun. It seemed silly. This wasn't much of a secret, and Kevin regretted missing his favorite TV show.

The man kept his hand on Kevin's knee as he drove, and when he was back into town he said, "I'll leave you off near your school. Is that all right?"

Kevin nodded and asked, "Where do you live?"

"Far away."

Kevin stood inside the kitchen door, knowing he had to wait for his mother's attention. He stood patiently, until she put the last mixing bowl in the dishwasher and dried her hands. She finally turned to him, read his look, and asked, "Why so serious?"

"Something's happened, I don't know."

"What's that, dear?"

It only took a few simple sentences to tell her and, as he spoke, she gripped the edge of the sink and stared at her beautifully ordered garden. It didn't take long to tell, because there was little about the experience that interested him. He just knew that it was oddly different. He simply wanted to know why.

She didn't ask him any questions because she knew what to do, what always worked in a world that was forever tumbling into disorder. She had to make her son clean. She took him up to the bath and scrubbed him. She used a whole bottle of disinfectant in the bathwater and her new vegetable brush. But she couldn't seem to get him clean enough, and she knew he had to be clean before his father came home.

Kevin sat in the burning water, too afraid to ask what was happening to him, too scared to cry. She had never been like this. He didn't dare look at her directly but stole glances, saw her mouth drawn taut and saw it was her very angriest mouth. What was scariest was that she wasn't telling him what he had done wrong. He just knew he must have done something awful, that it must be connected with the man. But now, for the first time in his life, his mother had no words for his transgression. He had stumbled into an immense sin too great for his mother to name. But there was always forgiveness by bedtime. He believed that, because it had always been that way, and then the awful scariness would go away.

Kevin loved airports. He was excited about seeing his Aunt Grace and his cousins, but disturbed about going alone and already missing his brother and sister. But he felt he was too big to tell his mother he was afraid. What made him most uneasy was that his mother kept assuring him that he was old enough to visit his aunt by himself, to get on a plane and find his seat and eat and find the bathroom.

She had taken him to the newsstand, where she'd said yes to every comic book he wanted, yes in that way she did when she was really telling him he was a nuisance, yes as a way to keep to herself and mind her own concerns.

She had been that way lately, always searching the air over his head, as if trying to remember something, the way she did in the supermarket when she forgot her list. But then a lot of things were different. He'd had no school or homework forever, and he felt his world had grown small and confusing. She had told him he wasn't well, but when he asked what he had, why he had to stay alone, she evaded with "Something. You've got something."

Not that he missed school and those boys in fourth grade who made his life miserable. But he couldn't help worrying about whether his picture of autumn leaves would get a gold star, as his picture of the airplane had.

Everything was so disturbingly different, like one of those movies he couldn't follow or those strained, silent dinners when his mother and father were arguing without saying anything. But some of the changes were wonderful, like airports and the smell of jet fuel and the latest issues of *Batman* and *The Green Lantern*.

At the security barrier his mother looked down at him and said, "Your Aunt Grace will meet you and they'll take good care of you on the plane. And don't you be any trouble to them."

"Uh-uh."

"And don't give your aunt any trouble about food. You eat what's put in front of you."

He nodded, not knowing what terrible things he might be expected to eat.

His mother walked toward a woman security attendant and said, "My son's on American Flight One Seventeen. Is there someone who can take him to the gate?"

The woman said, "Oh, I'm sure it will be all right for you to take him through. Won't it, Walt?" she asked the man next to her.

Claire said, "That won't be necessary. He's a big boy, aren't you, dear? I don't want to upset your routine."

The woman attendant looked curiously at Claire and said, "We're not busy. I'll see he gets to his gate and he's looked after."

"That's very kind of you. Go with the nice lady, Kevin," she said. She patted his cheek, stepped back, waggled her fingers at him, and hurried off.

She felt nothing, and that was the first relief she had had in days. He was gone, and her house no longer hummed with unspeakable anxieties. Her home was back in order.

She had called Grace from the airport to tell her his plane had left on time, and drove home to renew

order. She had so much to do, so much had been neg-
lected the last few days while she had wandered to sit
in every room of the house, hoping that in one of
them she would find peace or, she prayed, awake from
disorder.

Now he was gone and she was alone in her house
and she would have time to think and plan.

She started with the garden, weeding and spraying
with energy and then, order restored, had set upon the
house until it shined, the dirt of neglect expunged. She
felt her old energetic self. By the time she was satisfied
it was close to three, and she decided to reward her
good works with a few quiet minutes over coffee
before driving to pick up her children from the kind
neighbor who had taken them for the day.

It was good to have the house still again. Without
the constant whisper of the unthinkable, she could
again hear the murmur of those wonderful mecha-
nisms that shielded her family from heat and cold,
machines that cooked and cleaned and cooled. Now
she would be able to smell her cooking again. Her
senses were being restored. She felt well, grateful for
life, like someone emerging from illness. Thank God.
Even the sun spilling into her house was no longer
some false effect, some contradiction of reality.

She smiled at the day through her kitchen window,
and then she took her coffee cup and smashed it into
the sink with such force that the pieces shot up and
above her.

The awfulness had broken through again, and her
son was the medium for allowing horror into their lives.

And then she thought the unthinkable and unnatural: *God, forgive me, but I don't want him back.*

It was stress. She couldn't have thought that. She couldn't. She was a good mother. The thought was just an aberration. He was her son and she was a good mother.

She consigned her unnatural offense to God and forgetfulness.

He missed his brother and sister, but Cory and Debbie were exciting replacements when they weren't at school. His Aunt Grace was a nice lady, round and comfortable, with a soft voice and warm eyes. His uncle was like his father, not in looks but in the weighty authority he brought to a room. He toned things down, made Kevin quieter, slower of movement.

Grace started remembering tricks she had learned to keep a homebound child occupied and found that she enjoyed his lively company. She hadn't realized that she had grown a little lonely now that her own children were away all day, and she resumed her habit of keeping up a running dialogue with the child, not much caring if he paid attention, just feeling more cheerful by knowing her voice didn't float away into nothingness.

Now that Kevin was there, Claire called daily instead of twice a week, and their conversations were strictly kept to the familiar topics of family gossip and recipes and how much everything costs. But near the end of each call, without asking Claire, Grace would say "I'll let you talk to Kevin" and call, "Kevin, it's your mother. She wants to talk to you."

After the first two calls, Kevin came slowly to the phone, because his mother began by asking "I hope you're behaving yourself and not giving your Aunt Grace any trouble," to which he could only answer, "No."

"You be sure you don't, because it's very nice of her to have you there and you should be grateful." He would say, "Yes."

"Well, be a good boy and put your Aunt Grace back on." He'd hand the phone back to his aunt, who noticed how damp it was from his nervous hands.

Grace would say, "He's a dear and I love having him."

But at the end of three weeks, when Kevin handed the phone back to her, Grace said, "Kevin, be a darling and get me a Kleenex from the bathroom upstairs," and he raced off, anxious to please.

Grace said, "It's three weeks, Claire. I love having him and he's the best little boy in the world, but what about school? And you can't tell me you don't miss him."

"If he's getting to be a bother."

"I didn't say that. But how long can you keep him away?"

"You're right. He has to come home sometime. It's just that..."

"What?"

"I don't want to sound awful, but what if it happens again. What if somebody else... What I mean is, what if Kevin didn't tell us everything."

Grace's mouth snapped shut and she gave the

phone an exasperated shake. She sought a way to say what she needed to without setting Claire off and finally said, "Then you must ask him exactly what happened. Maybe you should have straight off."

"You know I couldn't. And what good would it do?"

Grace didn't know. Some good, surely, but she had to let the thought pass. She sensed the far-reaching emptiness implied in the willful pretense that silence would heal, but couldn't express it, didn't know how.

Kevin came hurrying down the stairs with her Kleenex, so she asked him to go into the yard, because she was sure she heard the neighbor's schnauzer, Jimbo, in the yard again. "Be a big help and shoo him out, dear."

Claire asked, "Is he gone?"

"Yes."

"When do you want to send him back?"

"Look, don't get mad, but I think you're going to have to sort this out sometime. You can't keep post-poning it. Maybe you should see someone."

"Someone? Don't you mean a psychiatrist?"

"Can you let it go on like this?"

"Yes, I can. I've thought about it. God help me, what else have I been thinking about? But there aren't any words for this. It's a cross, just something to bear, get past. Like Mom always said, 'Least said, soonest mended.' Just shut up and get over it as best you can. And I'm not going to tell strangers about what goes on in my family. You know very well what psychia-trists are; all they do is blame the parents. Well, we can't always be at fault. Dear Lord, we do our best. I certainly do. And then something like this happens and I won't let it be my fault."

And Grace knew from Claire's tone that the last words on the matter were being said. Forgetfulness would be commanded and enforced.

"When do you want to send him back?"

"I love having him."

"No, you're right. It's time the subject was closed. How about Friday? I'll call about flights and let you know."

The conversation petered out in strained banalities.

As she fixed dinner that night, Grace went over and over the troubling conversation. God, but Claire could drive you right up the wall. Talk about rigid. And then the disquieting thought came: What if there was more to what happened than Claire had told her? Maybe she should just sit Kevin down and talk to him herself, find out. No. Claire might find out.

She was snapped out of her reverie by a crash above that sent her rushing up to Cory's bedroom, where she found Cory and Kevin flailing on the bed. They were both in their underwear, and Kevin wore a towel for a cape. Captain Marvel was battling his dreaded nemesis, the archvillain Sivana, but in a painful flash she saw two boys and a terrible possibility.

She pulled Cory away and held him to her, protecting him and regretting what her fear implied.

Claire pulled the car into the driveway, got out, and took her son's suitcases from the trunk.

"Damned planes," she said as she tugged his bags

out and trudged up the walk, Kevin trailing. "Dinner's going to be late, but don't you dare eat anything beforehand. I'll fix something quick. Don't just stand there, get the door."

Kevin tugged it open to see his father standing just inside, near the foot of the stairs. He considered his son before smiling.

"Here's our world traveler," he said. "Plane late?" Kevin nodded, and his father said, "Now you know what I go through to make a living for you. Damned airlines."

Claire stood with the suitcases, and Kevin's father said, "Here, dear, I'll take them," cut around Kevin, took the bags, and headed up the stairs.

"Just leave them on his bed. I'll unpack them later. I've got to get right to dinner or we'll never eat," she said and hurried to the kitchen.

Kevin heard the sound of the television coming from the back room and knew that Dukey and Chrissy would be in front of it.

Kevin stood alone, feeling the way he did on the first day of school in a new classroom. New kids and new teachers, things to learn that would baffle him or that he was sure he could never learn or that he would learn and no one would ever ask him about again.

He stood alone, still in his coat, because he didn't know what he was supposed to do, where he should be or go. Everything felt wrong.

And then he knew what was out of place: No one had told him to wash up for dinner, and that wasn't right, that wasn't the way things had always been, were supposed to be.

He went up the stairs, past the closed door of his parents' room, and into the bathroom. Maybe if he was good and washed without being told... Maybe if he could be the best little boy that ever lived.

Magic

He glared at Donald Duck. Donald, looking more amiable than usual, stared blandly about, apparently ignoring him. Claude was in a sour mood and thought, *You're not the only one with a rotten temper, Donald.* Claude hadn't wanted to come to this joint, this...this monument to debased taste with its tons of numbing whimsy. He felt put upon, buried under a tidal wave of treacle. His mother had wanted to come, and now *she* was back at the hotel, having amused herself into exhaustion. She was "cuted" out. She'd cooed over too many marzipan buildings, exclaimed too many Ohs! and Ahs! as Mickey and Dopey and Chip and Dale waddled past, and almost clicked her Instamatic to meltdown.

Damn Walt Disney World! Damn his mother! Damn Donald Duck!

This is what one got for being the youngest son and single. She had five other boys, but he had to be the one to haul her to this Metropolis for Retards. Well, he'd get her shopping done for her and get out of here while he retained some measure of sanity.

He consulted his mother's list. There was something to be bought for each of her eleven grandchildren, and with the eye of the skilled shopper, his mother had remembered where she had seen each item, and her directions were meticulously precise. So far he had bought only the Daisy Duck tea service for Cheryl from the Emporium on Main St. His next stop was down the street at Disney & Co. to buy a pewter Mickey Mouse on ice skates for Chad.

He stormed off, grumbling that all her grandchildren were named after second-rate TV actors who were more famous for posters than performances. What else could he expect of his brothers and those women they'd married?

By noon he'd added the Dopey beach towel and the Mickey place mats to his purchases. He was hungry and murderous as he stood at the end of Main St., the sun slamming down and dark, wet rings spreading under the arms of his Sulka shirt. He winced as three women with terminal cellulite waddled past in shorts. Who were these people who bought armloads of ugly junk, ate on the run, and laughed with their mouths full? They were out of the same mold as his brothers and their families: They were everything he had given vast amounts of intense study and work toward *not* being. He thanked God he had gotten away from that lot, had become a man of some discrimination.

Hadn't he triumphed at Yale, been wooed by the best corporations, climbed General Electric's corporate ladder with surprising speed and agility? Wasn't he, at only thirty-one, a shrewd, even feared, vice president? He'd put his past behind him.

When asked where he had grown up, he answered "The Midwest" and gestured vaguely to encompass all that lay between the Hudson River and the Rockies. He was no longer from the Columbus, Ohio, that had nurtured and repelled him. Neither his mind nor spirit was any longer of Columbus. So what malign fate had condemned him to doing time here? His family's collusion and his own cowardice, that's what! The sibling chorus had caroled, "Mom hasn't spent time with you in years and she's been dying to go to Walt Disney World. You'd make her so happy if you went with her. *You were always her favorite.*"

No, his mind had cried. "Yes," his coward's tongue had said. How could a man who wielded so much corporate power have so little resistance to such brute manipulation?

He moved under a tree near the Crystal Palace restaurant, considering whether hunger wasn't preferable to eating surrounded by Styrofoam nostalgia, even if his stomach was making noisily shameful demands. He just wasn't used to simply *eating*. "Eating" was business and ceremony and impressing people.

But here he sat starving, watching a cosmeticized Snow White coo at children. He thought The Witch knew what she was doing when she went after that one. His stomach made a noise like a boulder flung in a river and, more to shut it up than anything else, he headed toward the Crystal Palace to see what the great unwashed were eating.

As he went, something red caught his eye, and he turned to see the most remarkably beautiful man standing near the entrance to the restaurant and looking his way. Claude stopped, struck still. The man in the red shirt was towering and slim, his head long and helmeted in coils of black curls, his sculptured face graced by an aquiline nose and a mouth carved from rose quartz. Their eyes met, and the man's crystalline aqua eyes pierced Claude and filled him with light. The force of their locked gazes bound them to each other, and its magnetism felt strong enough to lift them into each other's arms. Then five children ran jostling into Claude, screaming "Mickey! Mickey! Mickey!" their mother paddling in pursuit and shouting "Don't hurt Mickey."

Claude dodged out of their way, and when he looked up again the beautiful man was gone.

Where? There were no doors or alleys, and the man was much too tall to be lost in a crowd. Claude forgot he was hungry. The sight of another man had never so physically jolted him, and he suddenly felt bereft. Claude was astounded. This was irrational. After all, he had only seen the man, not even spoken. How could he feel like he'd lost someone he knew intimately?

He was no longer interested in food, but he ate to distract himself and to try to regain some sense of reality. Eating didn't work. He left the restaurant and went to linger where the man had stood. He finally, and sadly, went back to his mother's shopping list but did the job in a daze, not really seeing what he bought, as visions of the man seemed burned into his retina. He bought the Minnie Mouse T-shirt for Tweetie and the hologram of the space ship for Chucky, and between each purchase, he hurried back to stand near the Crystal Palace and turn like a lighthouse, beaming his gaze in every direction. By late afternoon he was back at the restaurant for the eighth time. The sun hung low behind Cinderella's Castle when, in the late-afternoon pink-gold light, the man reappeared exactly where he had first materialized. Claude dodged through the eddying crowds. He reached out and touched the man's shoulder, as much from necessity as the need to know he was real.

Claude said, "I thought I'd never see you again," and couldn't believe he had delivered such a banal line, but the man nodded and said, "I was afraid too. I hoped you'd come back. I knew you would. I've been here every time I could get away."

"This is the eighth time I've been back."

"I'm so glad you kept trying."

"I wish there was some place to have some privacy."

"C'mon," the man said and hurried off.

"Where are we going?" Claude asked, and the man answered, "Snow White's Adventure."

They walked quickly, staying close enough to brush arms and hands.

The man spoke to the attendant at the entrance, and they were waved ahead without having to wait on the long line. They boarded one of the moving gondolas, pressed close, and joined hands as they

traveled past the Huntsman raising his knife above
Snow White, the Dwarves hi-hoing, and the Witch
beguiling Snow White with the lethally red apple.
Their gondola clattered over the tracks as the fairy
tale unfolded on either side. Claude was enchanted
and felt this child's fantasy was wonderfully appropriate for their first intimacy and almost wept when a
symphony orchestra and a chorus burst into
"Someday My Prince Will Come."

The streetlights were on when they came out, and
the young man said, "I'm going to be late. I work here,
and they're tough about promptness. Tomorrow at ten,
in Liberty Square, up that way. Can you? It's important." He then added with painful urgency, "Isn't it?"

"Oh, yes," Claude answered.

The man started off, and Claude called, "What's
your name?"

"Peter Arden," the man called back.

Peter Arden! How beautiful. But his name would
have to be as lovely as he was, as his voice was.
Anything else would be unthinkable. As "Whistle
While You Work" spilled from a loudspeaker, Claude
was struck with the extraordinary idea that he had
invented this man, had summoned an illusion and
then, to suit some fantasy, given this magnificent
mirage a name.

No. Peter Arden was real. He just had to be.

To hell with the plane home tomorrow. He had
months worth of unused vacation time he'd passed up
in pursuit of his career. He would claim some time for
himself, have something that was all and only his.

Besides, it wasn't as if he had a choice; he felt as if his life depended on seeing Peter Arden again.

Peter Arden.

He bought the last item on his list, an expensive capo di monte tableau showing Snow White about to kiss Dopey on his bald head. His mother wanted it for her own mantel, and Claude didn't think unkind thoughts of her bizarre taste when he told the saleswoman where to ship it: He even sensed the delight his mother would take in it. What had seemed fraudulently tacky and dismayingly quaint now held, well, a modicum of charm.

He turned onto Main Street heading toward the exit. He struggled along with his purchases banging against his legs, but he felt jaunty and the turn-of-the-century street before him seemed an illuminated Wonderland of golden lights and exuberant gingerbread buildings. He felt as light and free as he had on his first pair of roller skates that had once carried him blocks from home into new realms and beyond the restraints of his watchful family. That wondrous sense of free flight had eluded him ever since. Now he seemed to whiz along on wheels.

The store windows he passed were full of amusements that made him smile and feel benevolent. He forgot his mean-spirited growl of two days ago when he first stood here and his mother said "Don't grind your teeth, Claude." Now his smile seemed to illuminate all it touched.

Peter Arden!

With a feeling of dazed elation he went into a

shop, removed his gold Rolex, and bought a Mickey Mouse watch that was just like the one he had loved as a child.

Pe-*ter* Ar-*den,* the watch ticked.

That evening Claude cajoled his mother into taking an earlier flight the next morning by dangling her grandchildren in front of her. Just think of their glowing faces, their chortling glee, when they saw "Nama"; saw what she, their fairy godmother, had brought from their favorite place in the whole world. Such joy! What bliss! Could she bear to wait? Could she delay seeing the tots upon whom she doted? As he went on with his seduction he felt guilty for being so blatantly manipulative. Well, turnabout was fair, wasn't it? If she knew where his buttons were, he also had the wiring diagram for hers.

He saw her off on an 8:30 flight, the earliest they had, then called his brother Henry to meet her.

Henry whined, "I just can't walk out of work and go get her."

"I can't make you get her, Henry. If you just want to leave your mother sitting in the airport, that's up to you."

"Why did she leave so early?"

"She just couldn't wait to see you and your family," Claude said and almost gagged on the lie. Give the guy a shot of guilt that would get his fat ass to the airport.

By 9:30 Claude was again on Main Street, feeling proprietary, smiling benignly on all he surveyed, like a kind monarch in a fairy tale who wanted only the best for his subjects. Had trees ever been as green or flowers as fresh and brilliant? He smiled at Snow White, who smiled back and bobbed her head. He saw Mickey Mouse and wanted to go pat him on his ballooning rump. He saw Goofy some distance away and watched as Goofy paddled along on his long flat feet, loose-armed, slack-jawed face thrust forward, marionette-like in his shambling movements. Claude was sure he heard him give his hiccoughing rube laugh as children crowded around him.

Claude checked his park map and hurried past the wilds of the Swiss Family Treehouse and the loquacious mechanical birds of Tropical Serenade, past jungles and pirates, finally making a sharp right into Colonial America where men in breeches collected debris with brooms and long-handled dustpans. He sat on the bench that circled the base of an oak facing where he was sure Peter Arden would appear.

As the clock atop the Hall of Presidents tolled ten, Peter was suddenly there, again seeming to emerge from a solid brick wall. It struck Claude as unsurprising that this extraordinary man should materialize from thin air.

As Claude neared him he saw that Peter's hair was crushed into a damp cap on his head, curls pressed wetly flat against a head as elegantly tactile as a Brancusi sculpture. His forehead was beaded with perspiration that made him glow. It took all Claude's self-restraint to keep from taking Peter's head in his hands and kissing him, for Claude lost almost all awareness of where he was when he looked at Peter.

"I had to run to get here on time," Peter said. "I don't have long."

"I just want to be near you awhile."

Peter nodded and started off, saying "The Haunted Mansion," and Claude followed along, knowing he would follow Peter anywhere.

Peter said, "It's dark and private and only two to a gondola. It's the most private."

Claude pushed down the idea that Peter seemed very expert on where one could have some privacy in the midst of crowds.

Again Peter dodged the line, and they were quickly in a gondola and immediately immersed in music and sound effects from the speakers mounted in the wings of the moving seats. As they rounded a bend in the dark, they kissed. Ghosts waltzed and a disembodied head intoned, but they knew nothing but closeness.

They walked back into the sun, their shoulders touching. Peter said "My God!" and Claude knew what he meant, that he was as bowled over by his feelings as he himself was, and Claude said, "I was due to go home today, but I'm staying. I have months of time coming to me. I never take any vacation. I'm never sick. I deserve some time. I have to see you later."

"Tonight," Peter said. "Can you pick me up?"

"Where?"

"At eight in the Daisy Duck lot nearest the drive to the entrance."

"And today?"

"It's hard to get away on my breaks, and I feel so

frustrated being near you without touching you."

"I know."

They confirmed their meeting, and Peter left Claude in front of the Christmas Shop.

Claude wondered how he would ever fill his day till he again saw Peter at Daisy Duck.

He went back to his hotel and called his office, begging illness and not much caring whether they believed him or not, and wondering how everything but Peter could seem so suddenly irrelevant, so immensely secondary, and Claude was sure Peter felt this as deeply as he did. He told his secretary to cancel his meetings for the next few days, as well as his flights to Hong Kong and Taiwan and Munich. No, he was feeling very ill and he didn't know when he would be able to return to work.

Claude filled out his day at Sea World and found everything there delightful, in an abstracted way. He ate lunch and, five minutes after leaving the restaurant, couldn't remember what he had eaten. As he gazed down into a tank and saw a seal swim near, he felt a compulsion to leap in and hug it. When he watched the dolphins leap twenty feet into the air he felt as free and airborne as they must, and tears ran down his cheeks. He didn't know that madness could feel so sweet and poignant and elating and profoundly sad, and all at the same time.

Their dinner was eaten mostly in silence in a restaurant chosen after several tries at finding one that offered some privacy. They found one with booths that closed others out and them in. They stared at each other, feeling a little awed by the suddenness, the power, and the rightness of their discovery.

When conversation came it was in thin, unadorned slices. Not that they weren't interested, but vital statistics—hometown, schools, parents, brothers, sisters—felt irrelevant. So little was said that they might have been taken for people who had known each other for years and can afford silence. From time to time they reached and touched hands under the table. They said no to desserts as the waitress removed their barely touched entrées.

Sex in Claude's brightly lit hotel room was merely an extension of what they'd been experiencing. Claude, jaded by brief encounters that were more therapeutic and expedient than passionate, felt vividly alive under Peter's hands. Peter, always shy, felt daring and unrestrained and safe with Claude. Mind and emotions were joined and completed with their bodies, and both sensed the newness of it. They finally lay in a tumble of limbs and sheets, forehead to forehead, and peered into each other's eyes. Words were still unnecessary, and neither seemed willing to break an almost sacred silence.

Finally, his eyes millimeters from Peter's, Claude—not imagining that people were born here—asked, "How did you get down here to Orlando?"

"My agent. I'm an actor and singer," Peter answered.

"I'd love to see you. I'm sure you're wonderful."

MAGIC

"This is the best job I ever had. I just love being Goofy."

"We're all different, all special." Claude misunderstood.

"No. I mean, I'm really Goofy."

"And kind and warm and affectionate."

Peter pulled back and sat up. "No, like, I mean, that is, Goofy in the cartoons. For real. Well, not for real. I dress up like him and go out in the park and meet the kids."

Claude stared hard at Peter's beautiful face, as if he expected to see Peter's ears grow long, lank, and black. He said with a twist in his voice, "You mean it."

"I love it. Well, the suit's hot and makes me sweat, but the looks on the kids' faces are something. They've seen me...I mean this guy...for years on television and in movies and, *bang!* There he is in the flesh. Mickey is everybody's favorite, next to Donald and Dopey, of course, but they really like me, because they're not in awe of this dumb guy. He's someone they can be friends with."

Claude fought down panic, because Peter felt suddenly blisteringly hot to his touch. He snatched back his hand, rose, and hurried into the bathroom where he gripped the edge of the sink and stared unseeing at his stricken reflection in the mirror. Peter's news was staggeringly impossible. Claude felt that a social and intellectual Matterhorn had been thrust up before him. And he felt afraid; no, terrified. He realized that he had been willing to overthrow important work for a passionate whim and had been so hypnotized, so infatuated, that

95

he hadn't even been aware of what he was doing. He'd been following a Pied Piper, running after seductive music toward an abyss. My God, he had been willing to forego advantage for a man whose only accomplishment was to play a stupid cartoon character, and a gawky stupid one at that.

What had be been thinking to just cavalierly shunt his important work aside to be with Peter, to just have passionate, incredible sex with Goofy? He, a young vice president of an international corporate giant, had acted like a lovesick fool. He who already reached a height with a good view of vast divisions he might soon run. He who had already been interviewed by *Fortune* and *Forbes* reporters who described him as one of the world's youngest movers and shakers. He who had his shirts made at Turnbull and Asser, his suits on Saville Row, and his hair dressed at Trumper's. Suites at the Beverly Hills Hotel and the Peninsula in Hong Kong. He was where multitudes wanted to be.

Claude slumped onto the toilet. Of course there were the nights when there wasn't enough work to take him to midnight. Now and then he might pace his five-room condo as if he had mislaid sleep. So what if there were nights when exhaustion was no longer enough to let him sleep? So what if he needed the occasional call boy? Tough! Tough shit! It was worth it. And here he was loitering in fucking Orlando doing something very out of character and undoubtedly stupid.

All this nonsense for transient pleasure with some man with no goal in life beyond dressing as a dim-witted dog.

He'd be damned if he'd go on making a fool of himself. He must think of some excuse to get rid of Whatsisname. He had to get moving, make some calls to set his real life in motion. It was probably too late to get a plane out tonight, but if he left early enough tomorrow he might still make the Taiwan meeting and could backtrack to the earlier one in Hong Kong and then get on to Germany. He might even manage a weekend in London. Peter might be a little hurt, but in the long run it would certainly be better for both of them. He'd fired a lot of people in his time, and he knew the trick was not to look them in the eye and see what it was costing them.

Claude stood erect and felt on firmer footing, and then felt his resolve begin to unravel. *This is impossible and absurd,* he scolded himself. *Get the hell out of here. Prince Charming, maybe. Goofy, never.*

Peter knocked and asked, "Are you all right?"

Claude intended to say very brightly "Fine," but he startled himself by answering "No."

Peter tried the door and found it locked. He said anxiously, "What's the matter? Do you need help?" and Claude surprised himself by saying, "Everything's the matter and I don't want any help."

"Are you sick? Open the door."

"I can't."

There was a pause before Peter said, "Sure you can. I'm here."

Claude opened the door. No long black ears, no snout, no black jellybean nose. Just beautiful Peter and confusion, and too many feelings and, suddenly, tears.

Peter held Claude as Claude wept.

Claude wanted to make a wish as he had as a child, to clench his fists at his sides and stand stiff, to gasp in great draughts of air and then, with all his might and main, to hurl his wish at heaven, to shatter the sky and have his wish come pouring down on him.

After all, this was the Magic Kingdom, so why not make a wish? And why shouldn't it come true?

He held Peter as if he might fall off the world if he let go and wished harder than he ever had for things he hadn't known he wanted.

Eluding Fame

One of the main troubles was that everyone had an opinion. Everyone knew what was "right" for Charles to do or not do. Of course, it was really no one's business but his, but we all got sucked into the debate, probably because there wasn't much else going on in our own lives, so mucking about in Charles's took up the slack.

It started when Charles was going to have the first exhibit of his paintings in eighteen years at the Flexner Gallery. The gallery was new and had attracted a great deal of attention. Better yet, it found buyers, not offering the latest sensations in art but by tracking down the forgotten artists of the twenties and thirties and displaying them in lush surroundings in a townhouse in the East Sixties, just off Fifth Avenue.

By luck or prescience, the gallery capitalized on the reaction against new "schools" of art that began to seem more and more absurd despite volumes of scholarly articles and support. Signed urinals, sinks, bricks, and rags were still showing at better galleries and selling well, but there was a renewed market for the readily recognizable—for "representational" art, as it was dubbed.

Over the decades, Charles had gone from being a sensation of the pre-WWII art world to a minor footnote, pursuing and mastering a manner of painting called Magic Realism. Charles hated the term because it lumped him with others in a "school" he hadn't signed up for. More to the point, Charles didn't like most other painters and avoided them. For him, painting was a solitary pursuit, like praying.

As years passed, Charles absorbed the pain of the public's neglect, ignored artistic fashions, and got on with the only work he loved and that seemed to love him back. Every day of the week he sat at his battered card table over a gesso panel and painted, laying layers of oil paint down with tiny brushes, building a color in layers until it gathered depth and seemed to glow from within. He had learned all-but-forgotten painting techniques and could capture the whole of the Piazza Navonna on a board the size of a sheet of paper and in a manner that forced the viewer to see more that a photo or even the place itself revealed. When he painted a velvet coat it was tactile and his flowers lacked only scent. He *saw* in the way that musical prodigies *hear.* A visit to an art gallery with him left me feeling half blind, as he pointed out details and remarked on techniques my eye could barely see.

He painted against fashion and, except for a few

collectors, almost fell from sight. If he was a magnificent oak falling in an uninhabited forest, he didn't seem to mind. It was his friends who resented it.

Thanks to the generosity of a former lover, Charles was made fairly rich and was freed from the financial uncertainty that had dogged him. When the inheritance came, his friends expected a self-indulgent spree, but he'd spent so many years just squeaking by that he had lost the habit of money. He spent what he had on friends and charities.

Charles eased into old age with much of what most people long for: He had money, peace of mind, good friends, and work he loved.

Then, as will happen, he lived long enough to come back into style. And that's where the trouble started, mostly thanks to Hamish Burgoyne's getting it into his head that, finally, Charles could have his due after all the neglect. Hamish had the means for lavishing public attention on Charles.

Hamish Burgoyne (not his real name, but Hamish rightly preferred it to Louis Stumphill) was editor in chief of *Art-Retro*, a new magazine that exhumed the reputation of painters from the twenties and thirties who all topped sixty or had already died in both deserved and undeserved oblivion. Almost single-handedly, *Art-Retro* revived interest in pictures of things and places one could easily recognize, and the magazine was proving a great success, even at twenty dollars per copy. The articles that accompanied the illustrations were full of gossip about the artists' intimate lives, including detailed accounts of their sexual proclivities, lovers, and assorted psychoses. All in all, the magazine was a prurient, glossy, costly example of show and tell-all. Its detractors were few but vocal, such as one sniffy critic who said, "The rotten magazine makes it sound as if the old crocks had been painting with their dicks." Hamish wasn't offended and said, "If I had pictures of that, I could double circulation."

Hamish genuinely admired Charles's work and over the years had bought five of his paintings and was an active booster of the work. Hamish was always pained when other collectors couldn't see the brilliance. Now, with his magazine, Hamish would prove his judgment had been very *avant* in a *retro* way. As they say in crime novels, Hamish had "motive, means, and opportunity." He could see to it that Charles was lionized and recognized. Hamish meant well, and that was the problem. Meaning well usually involves doing the unwanted for the unwilling, leaving both parties very pissed off. How do you tell someone who insists on doing something "good" for you to mind his own damned business?

Hamish planned to devote the major portion of the October issue of *Art-Retro* to Charles, to coincide with the opening at the Flexner Gallery. The cover illustration would be the painting of Hadrian's Villa, and there would be sixteen pages of full-color reproductions and a ten-page article. Hamish knew a lot about Charles, the influences on his work (the Caribbean, Italy, Botticelli, Ingres) and even more about Charles's sex life and lovers (Charles's patron Claude, four major lovers of some duration, and dozens of others who were barely given time enough to muss the sheets). The cover caption would read: CHARLES RAND: RESTORED GLORY FOR A MASTER.

However, Hamish didn't consult Charles. It was to be a surprise. Hamish saw his gesture as that of a beneficent angel of the arts who, single-handedly, would raise Charles from obscurity.

I didn't know any of this until Hamish called me in April to ask to borrow one of my paintings by Charles.

"What for?" I wanted to know. "I've promised it to Charles for his show in October."

"I'll only need it for a month or so."

"For what?"

"Now, don't tell Charles, but I'm planning an issue that will feature him. Actually, the bulk of the issue will be about him."

"He doesn't know?"

"He'll be beside himself."

"He'll be up your ass. There's nothing he likes less than surprises. He almost walked out on that birthday party Henry gave him. Do you remember the look on his face?"

"This is different. He'll love this. So, how about loaning me the picture?"

"I don't know."

"You can be a terrible poop."

"I know, but I think you should talk to Charles."

"Charles will be ecstatic. Don't you think it's time he stopped hiding his light under a bushel?"

"It's his light."

"Well, he shouldn't do it, and I've told him so. What's the sense of painting for a handful of people? Anyway, what about loaning me the picture?"

"If Charles knows."

His sigh crackled in the phone and he said, "Just don't tell Charles anything. Let me do it in my own good time."

"Of course," I said, and felt uneasy.

Hamish and I went back a long way, to public schools in Schenectady and the same working-class neighborhood. It made Hamish wary of me. He was always sure I'd start talking about the not so good old days, as if there was anything memorable or interesting to say about Schenectady. While I was rather proud of getting out of there, Hamish saw his origins as demeaning and didn't want them recalled. Hamish preferred to see himself as sprung fully formed from the brow of Zeus. After all, he'd gone from wearing Fruit of the Loom drawers from Woolworth's to Bergdorf's best Egyptian cotton underwear and a laundress who came in once a week to iron them to wrinkle-free perfection. But, to give him credit, he had made himself a force in the art world and was shrewd and successful in promoting himself and the artists he believed in.

It was late May before Hamish made public his plans for the article on Charles. He should have presented the idea to Charles in private but, with astonishing miscalculation, he chose to do it during a dinner Charles was hosting at La Choix for the seven of us who made up what I dubbed "Rand's Raiders." It was Frank's birthday, I think, but we really didn't need a reason for getting together. We saw a lot of each other because we never seemed to run out of things to talk or laugh about.

We were sitting over cocktails and menus when Hamish tapped his glass (irritating!), and everyone turned to him with puzzled expressions. He began, "I have a surprise for Charles, and I hope he'll be as pleased as I am. Charles's show is in October, and that month's issue of my magazine is going to be devoted almost entirely to him and his work. We already have the layouts, and I've written the article myself."

Charles's face knotted, but Hamish was too full of himself to notice and he plunged on. "I've never enjoyed writing anything more. God, but didn't it bring back memories; Claude and how wonderfully generous he was to Charles. And I hadn't thought of Phil in ages. Wasn't he beautiful? You were together for seven years, weren't you? Well, Charles, just correct me. And then there was Chris and your first trip to Italy and all the wonderful pictures that came out of that. And the Verona paintings, the Villa d'Este, Hadrian's Tomb. And that lovely Hugh and the flower pictures. My piece is excellent, if I do say so myself."

Hamish clattered along, sipping his martini by way of punctuation. He still hadn't noticed the look on Charles's face, which was as well, as it would have turned him to stone. Hamish wound down and finally gave Charles his full attention, expecting to see Charles glowing with gratitude. Charles's glow was more like that of an overheated furnace.

Charles was the most scrupulously courteous person I've ever met, and I saw him struggling to compose his face and a reply. He was finally able to strain out, "How kind of you to think so well of my work." His words were polite and well below freezing.

Hamish started to speak, and Charles began ostentatiously looking for our waiter. We all felt the chill. Hamish looked like a schoolboy who was sure of an A and found himself expelled. Several efforts at conversation sputtered in strained silences, and we broke up early, relieved to be out of each other's company.

The next day phone calls ricocheted among the friends, and the curtain went up on a small intense drama we all watched and performed in.

As the phone calls were exchanged, the themes of the drama emerged.

Frank felt that what Hamish offered Charles was wonderful, an overdue vindication of great talent. Frank would, because Frank dearly wanted Charles to have the fame Frank had pursued for himself. As a young man, Frank had debuted on Broadway and had been marked by everyone as an actor of elegant promise. The promise was never kept. Not unusual, but no less painful and forever baffling for Frank. Paramount and Twentieth had made screen tests and found the camera barely noticed him. The studios didn't even bother to call to say he wasn't wanted. He proved a fine reliable stage actor but not the stuff of stars. Consulting his old wounds, Frank believed that Charles must want the recognition. Charles must ache—as Frank did—for final vindication of his talent, even if it came late. For fame was a lover, and wasn't it wonderful to be loved at any age?

Dick and Kenny were older than Charles and had always been like kind and benevolent uncles to him and, even though they were all old now, Charles was still deferential to them and trusted their judgment. But in this case, their judgment was shaped by over four decades of hiding their relationship. They still had separate bedrooms and believed only a few of their straight friends knew the truth of their union. Their straight friends colluded in the fraud.

They argued against the article ever appearing and were sure that Charles too must be repelled by the idea of revealing "matters best kept private." Not that they'd read the article, but they knew the magazine and the thrust of its pieces; prurience piled on scandal wrapped in notoriety. It wasn't done. It was beyond the pale. Scandalous. The words they used to describe their attitude were dated but conveyed their outrage as newer words would not have. They couldn't stand the idea of their beloved friend being exposed to such onerous attention. As they said, "Charles's work is not cheap. Why should it be debased by an article no better than the trash in *The National Enquirer?*"

Striking the contemporary note was Johnny, who was a consultant to an advertising agency on marketing to gays. Johnny felt that every gay person should be out, that it was a lie to let others live with the illusion one was straight. Johnny wanted to haul Charles to the Stonewall barricades. Wouldn't it be wonderful for Charles to finally come out and become a role model, and to give the finger to the world at large? Fuck what other people thought. Once Charles was famously out, Johnny might even get him space ads for upscale products. It's hard to imagine what Johnny had in mind: "Distinguished artist Charles Rand brushes with Colgate"? Unlikely. Johnny said all this to Charles in his up-tempo, to-the-ramparts voice. Johnny felt he had more influence on Charles than the rest of us because Charles and he had sex from time to time. However, in this case, Johnny's erection wasn't the right lever.

I didn't express my opinion, not because there seemed to be more than enough going around; I just couldn't seem to arrive at one. I listened to the arguments and tried to balance what was good and bad about each, but I couldn't come down on one side or the other. What I felt was that Charles's work was truly brilliant and deserved a public, but I wasn't sure the magazine would do that for him.

It was a mark of Charles's exceptional courtesy that he even listened to all the unasked-for advice. All he ever said was "You may be right," leaving the hearer to believe what he wanted.

But one night I arrived at his apartment ahead of everyone else and Charles answered the door in tears. I didn't know what the matter was, but I put my arms around him and held him, which seemed to make things worse, as he began to sob. All I could think to do was hold him and pat him until he calmed a little.

He moved out of my arms and I fished a tissue from my pocket to give him.

I asked, "What's the matter?" and he turned away and shrugged.

"Can I help?" He shrugged again and again. I asked, "What's the matter?"

He finally spoke: "I can't paint. Haven't been able to in weeks. All this fuss. I don't want it. I don't."

He pushed the very damp tissue into his pocket and asked, "What would you like to drink?"

I followed him into the kitchen.

I asked, "Is it that damned article?"

Charles flapped his hand helplessly.

"Well," I said, "who wants his dirty linen hung in public, even if it is for the sake of art?"

I put my arm over his shoulders.

"Tell Hamish no. Tell him you don't want your dirt dished up. If he wants to run pictures, fine. Otherwise, no."

Charles bobbed his head. Tears were still running, so I pulled a paper towel from the roll and blotted him.

That evening I was sure I understood what he must be feeling. He was too old to come out. He'd learned the lessons of repression in a time when it was dangerous to be out. I knew his history and I'd been close to him for a long part of it.

He'd fled his Midwest hometown because he was too blatantly himself and couldn't seem to find a suitable disguise. His embarrassed father had ponied up the money for Charles to go to Germany and study painting, implying strongly that there was no need for him to hurry back.

Charles arrived in Berlin in time to see Hitler strut to power. One day Hitler was scheduled to drive down the avenue where Charles was living in a *pensione*. Charles decided to entertain the troops by improvising a costume of Carmen. Rose in teeth, lips rouged, fringed scarf over his head, he hung out his window and waved and called to the goose-stepping soldiers, until the two Jewish sisters who owned the *pensione* ran into the room and hauled him from the window. In less than a year, Berlin grew too oppressive and the Nazi gangs that stalked the streets beat some of his gay friends. He returned to New York and joined the thousands of other men who had fled there to establish their own gay nation.

Not that New York was entirely hospitable to gays in the thirties, but they didn't send them to concentration camps. And in Manhattan, an entire illegal society flourished behind a veil.

I met Charles in 1960. My age put me on the cusp between Charles's generation and Stonewall, so I was with Charles when we were refused tables at restaurants ("We don't serve your kind here") or when sneering remarks were made in stores, at the theater, or on the street. Corrosive drops of disdain meant to wear away respect. Stonewall came in time for me and too late for Charles. Being exhorted to grab a rainbow flag and march scared the hell out of most of the older men I knew. When I marched in the first gay pride parade, the reaction of my older friends was fear—but oddly, mostly for themselves. "What if someone saw you?" they asked.

A couple of days after I found Charles crying I heard that he had canceled his October show at the gallery and, a day later, that Hamish had cancelled his feature on Charles and hastily cobbled together an issue on Reginald Marsh.

Charles went back to painting pictures only a handful of people saw, but he seemed his old self. He went to Tiffany and bought Hamish an elegant set of cuff links that he sent with a note Hamish showed me. It read: "Thank you for your thoughtful effort. Sorry it didn't work out. Charles."

Years went by and Charles became terminally ill with colon cancer. He was calm and orderly in arranging his affairs. His money had made money and he was able to fund the building of a wing in a fine museum in his hometown. The only provision of his gift was that, for one month each year, they would mount a show of his work. During his last months he began tracking down his paintings and was able to buy back many that he bequeathed to the museum.

Charles's last year of life was full of an agony that, most of the time, he managed to hide. Once, when he must have desperately needed someone to know what was really going on, he told me he would come home and stalk his apartment, crying out in pain, but worrying about whether his screams disturbed his neighbors. Another time he told me about coming home from lunch and just making it into his apartment before fouling himself. It shamed and scared this fastidious man.

His last month was spent bedridden at home. He was released from the hospital and made his executor promise not to send him back. Round-the-clock nurses took over the living room.

Charles was heavily drugged, but I'd sit with him for a while every day. Sometimes he seemed alert, sometimes becalmed in a narcotic haze. Before I visited I would try to think of what I might tell him that he would find interesting, until I realized that the sound of my voice and presence was all that mattered.

A couple of days before he died he seemed calmer and less pained than usual, and more lucid.

When the nurse left us alone, I gave him a kiss. He asked, "Does that mean we're engaged?" I laughed at our old joke and was glad he was feeling better.

I held his hand and we sat in silence for a while, until he said, "All that terrible business."

"About what?" I asked.

"That show, that article by Hamish."

"Oh, that was ages ago. Why bother yourself?"

"I keep thinking about it. I should have let him. He meant well. The problem was that I had everything I wanted. I could paint what was important to me. It was always about painting. That's all. And then everyone started in on me and I couldn't work. I think the truth was that I was afraid of the critics. They can hurt. I learned that early. I couldn't face that. What if they said I'd wasted all those years of work? It wouldn't have made the work any better or worse, but I was afraid it might keep me from going on."

I saw truth in what he said, but I never could believe it was the whole truth. And that's what has nagged me all these years.

If Charles had learned to be protective of his art, he had also learned to protect his secret. To face critics might be daunting, but facing society must have seemed a monstrous obstacle.

And to "face" society about what? Being gay? Being gay was probably the least interesting thing about my extraordinary friend.

ANATOMY LESSON

His whang was the stuff of classic Greek comedy. Athenians would have loved Jim's dick, painted it rampant on their vases and on the walls of taverns and bordellos. They would have immortalized his schlong and lionized him. Aristophanes would have found inspiration in Jim's pud and, for once, could have put the real thing onstage, instead of the clumsily made prop pricks that served his actors.

Unfortunately, Jim and his tool were born into this century in 1926, only twenty-three years after Queen Victoria's death, in an age when what he chose to do with it seemed to be not his business but everybody else's. So, as a man of his century, he was denied acclaim and his endowment was merely a matter of covert comment and ribaldry, and the quarry of passionate pursuit. His life illustrated the adage that "anatomy is destiny." It was Jim's fate to be tugged about by his member. It worked much the way a divining rod does, vibrating and leading the diviner on. It was thus that Jim's dick gave proof to another old saw: A stiff prick has no conscience...and less sense.

When Jim reached his sixties and looked back over his life, he pretty much concluded that he had done a lot more for his dong than it had ever done for him. But, given his titanic tool, it was almost impossible to imagine how life might have been different for him. Few men could, or would, have behaved differently.

His difficulties started in the maternity ward, after his birth in early February 1926, in Locus, Kan., a farm community of a few hundred dedicated Christians.

Most baby boys have little stubs that don't look like much more than an outsy belly button or a tea rose, but it was obvious to the maternity nurses that nine-pound, ten-ounce Baby Jim's member was well on its way to being a good deal more than what Nurse Jennings called "parlor size." Dr. Kerns, who performed Jim's circumcision, looked at it wryly and shouted over the baby's wails, "All the damned thing needs is pubic hair."

When his deeply religious Baptist mother, Mrs. Cloris Fandel, first unwrapped him to change his diaper she was horrified. She knew she had a boy, but this was entirely too much boy. Baby Jim had been dutifully conceived without her ever having to lay eyes on her husband's "you know what," and here she was faced with a baby that was dauntingly adult "down there." Baby Jim made her grateful she had never before laid eyes on the male appendage and that during her toils toward conception she had hummed hymns in her head while her husband labored over what felt to him like a warm ironing board.

She hated changing the baby. She would avert her eyes and unpin him, tears of embarrassed frustration seeping. It was unseemly. Worse, she came to think of it as God's judgment on her, and she completely lacked even a run-of-the-mill sinner's imagination. Still, her religion told her God sent woes, ills, frogs, and boils to test and punish. She saw Jim's member as her cross, which led her to a rare form of Christian confusion.

Because his mother tried to keep him tidy without having to look at what she was doing, Baby Jim was as sloppily diapered as a blind Hindu and bore as many random safety-pin puncture marks as a spastic junkie.

Appalled by this gross evidence of maleness, Jim's mother never gave him a brother or sister but did give his father short shrift and a twin bed, and gave all her passion to disciplining doilies to lie flat, to tracking dust bunnies, and to other decent Christian pursuits. As for Jim's father, Simon, he never demonstrated the least stress over her conjugal denial, as long as Miss Wurtzel worked in his hardware store.

His mother forced Baby Jim's toilet training hastily and harshly, and he could bathe himself, if haphazardly, when he was little more than two. When he could toddle, his mother put him in Jockey shorts and, because they were not made for children as young as he, cut them down and assured the desired modest restraint by sewing an extra panel of thin muslin into the fly.

She sewed badly and gave Baby Jim the appearance of a potbelly. His mother said it was baby fat. Let people think what they wanted, because it was sweet balm to her soul to see him as neutered as a Sears underwear ad.

With a degree of wary watchfulness that would have awed Torquemada, Jim's mother was able to keep her (and his) shameful secret until his teens.

As Jim grew older, he didn't prove anything special in school or the community, nor were his looks more than amiably neutral. He was one of life's "extras," barely noticed behind those who fill the world's foregrounds and get the close-ups. He had sandy hair with blond highlights, blue-gray eyes, and he stopped growing when he achieved the American all-purpose norm of 38 regular. His private distinction was not even indicated by a Cyranolike nose, pendulous earlobes, a strangler's thumbs, or size fifteen shoes.

Because his mother never let him go swimming with other boys, his noble knob remained his secret until an early September Monday after his first outing as a member of the Locus High freshman basketball team.

After their first practice session the team retired to their cramped locker room, where Jim undressed timidly, if with immense curiosity, because he was finally going to see another human naked. Was his body like other boys, or would he prove, when nude, to have less of this or more of that, or even find he was lacking something vital? Was he supposed to have only one penis and two balls? He knew bulls did, but what about boys? It didn't take him long to realize that, in one respect, the other boys were miniature copies of himself.

When he was sure he had everything the others had, he tugged off his shorts and hastily covered himself with his towel as he dashed for the shower room.

He entered the crowded steamy room to the sound of the raucous ribaldry of boys being boys. Of course, as in any male shower, the newcomer's appendage was covertly inspected, his endowment assessed. Henry Busch grabbed the first sidelong glance at Jim and gasped "Golly!" drawing everyone's attention to where he was gawking. The boys stopped showering and stared. Their expressions were much like those of the crowd in *It Came From Outer Space;* a remarkable alien had landed among them, and they responded with a mixture of awe, reverence, and fear. Their first instincts were to cover themselves, to spare their woefully adequate endowments the shame of comparison. Walter Grumbach—who, until Jim, had been Cock of the Walk—ceded his "crown" to Jim by whispering a reverential "Holy shit!"

What made the sighting even more awesome was that Jim's dong was apparently quiescent, lazily swaying like an elephant's trunk sniffing the ground for peanuts.

Jim hung his head shyly, but he was smiling a goofy Alfred E. Newman "What, me worry?" smile, sensing that something of moment was happening. He hadn't known he was *that* special. He had already gotten much pleasure from himself but hadn't known that most boys needed only one hand or, sadly, a couple of fingers, while he found two hands more useful, and fun. And in that steamy setting, three perceptions began to change Jim's life: For one, he found the distinction he hadn't even known he longed for from his peers. For another, he began to nurture the feeling that his member was the main, if not the only, reason people would find him interesting. His third insight was that he was disturbingly stirred by the sight of the other boys' nakedness, an insight that revealed itself further when he bolted from the shower room, his towel billowing before him like a schooner's sail.

Farm boys have a rustic sophistication about sex that is denied most city children. They grow up around animals and learn early the sexual delights of liver and melons and the tantalizing dangers of milking machines. But for all their practical knowledge, Jim was able to enlarge their sense of sexual possibilities. His fellows saw him as bringing distinction to his class, even to all of Locus. They felt his largeness spoke well of the manly qualities of Locus's males and of what their town was capable of producing. A sign at the city's border might proclaim Locus as "America's Cornmeal Capital," but there wasn't a boy in Jim's class that wouldn't have changed the sign to honor Jim if he could figure out how to word it. As it was, the best their imaginations could conjure was a nickname bestowed not humorously but in admiration: Jim was nicknamed "The Locus Longhorn." He hated it but sensed it was intended to honor and distinguish him, so he learned to smile when it was aimed his way.

Soon after his debut in the shower, a delegation of boys was able to talk him into displaying his whanger in full whang. Several *Wow!*s were exclaimed, and Jim smirked at his audience as it rose majestically above a pair of rosy brown pendants somewhere in size between tennis and golf balls. On that premiere day Nathaniel Sanmeyer, who would become Jim's first lover, almost fell to his knees from passionate trembling, experiencing a kind of religious epiphany that would eventually lead him into a monastery. The few "fast" girls who heard rumors of Jim's largeness pursued him with ardent curiosity but, though movies, books, ads, and his classmates told Jim he was supposed to be interested in girls, he couldn't summon more that a courteously remote interest.

Jim passed out of high school and into the navy, barely noticing the transition. Once again he was granted a kind of gleeful awe and treated to endless coarse humor. He was never lonely in the shower, never without free drinks in bars, and never able to bring himself to do anything sexual while in the navy.

He proved nothing special as a sailor, being assigned mostly to office chores at a base hospital. His single ward assignment was as a "snapper" (his term) in a circumcision recovery ward, an always-full room, because the navy preferred its men unsheathed in 1948. Jim's job was to keep an eye on the bandaged "wursts," and if he saw one becoming aroused, he was to rush over and give it a sharp flick on its underside with his index finger fired from his thumb. The target subsided immediately and the stitches remained intact. Not a single dong suffered from torn stitches under Jim's catlike attention, and the surgeon commended him for his devoted attention to his duties.

Otherwise, his navy service was uneventful and he was mustered out, leaving nothing behind but stories told by career men of this guy with the ten-pound tool.

Despite his navy years of self-enforced celibacy he was not naive, and moved immediately to San Francisco, intent on resuming his sexual education. The first trick he fished out of a bar on Castro Street was all it took for the joyful news of Jim's lob to be proclaimed far and wide. After that Jim could have put a meter on his bed and made his fortune. Instead, he chose to become knowledgeable and to learn about what, and who, he liked in bed. Somewhat to his chagrin, he developed a taste for men with removable upper plates (no abrasions) and a dislike for men with foxy jaws and overbites. While his equipment led some to an anatomical impasse, most rose to the occasion, feeling faintly heroic at coming to grips with the challenge.

But after a year or so of exploration, he began to tire of the passing parade, of names on matchbook covers and damp cocktail napkins, and started to long to settle down. He began looking for a lover, but over the next few years none seemed to suit him, either lacking this or in need of that. Tom wanted sex in the morning (prior to oral hygiene), Dick wanted passion while decked out in Frederick's of Hollywood, and Harry wanted it at night with the shades up and the lights on. The "auditioning" lovers drank too much or not enough. They didn't rinse the sink after shaving. They forgot to water houseplants. Eventually, they just wouldn't do, and years of fleeting passions marched over his mattress.

They came. They went. But neither their comings nor their goings made much of a ripple in Jim's life, and Jim might have gone serenely on in this way if he hadn't had the misfortune of falling desperately in love with a man named Herbert.

Three months of Heaven followed their meeting. They were as one. Jim fit Herbert in every way and place.

The two were remarkably alike. Neither desired to be noteworthy; neither longed for more than could be had with a modicum of effort or for more than casual comforts. And both saw secure retirement as a sensible, sufficient goal. They had everything. In their first week together they looked for an apartment to share and, as they planned living together, they were overjoyed to find they agreed on paint colors and fabrics, rug textures and paintings, casserole recipes, even brands of paper towels and cake mixes. It was not the stuff of grand passion or myth, but they were enormously happy and delighted with each other on a mattress that didn't seem likely to survive its warranty.

From their first night together—when they *knew*— they vowed to be faithful to each other. But to his surprise, Jim soon found that his love for Herbert made him incredibly horny for everyone but Herbert, and he became tortured by his ambivalence. He wanted Herbert desperately, needed the spiritual order he found with Herbert, but was desperately unsettled by being settled.

He harangued himself for his duplicity and tried to figure out why happiness made him so promiscuously horny. Was it that he needed a crowd of admirers? Did he long for the looks of nakedly greedy desire a flash of his pud evoked? Did he want to hurt his lover? Was he, at heart, cut out only for a randily solitary life of one-nighters? He found no answers, for he had no talent for introspection; all he knew was that he had never ached to play the satyr until Herbert. Perversely, Jim could estimate his love for Herbert, measure for measure, by his increasingly compulsive need for tea rooms, parks, meat racks, bars, alien beds, alleys, cars (parked and moving), bus and other transportation terminals, and public places of dangerous inventiveness. He loved and needed the strangers' expressions of slack-jawed voraciousness when he unzipped and began to uncoil, snaking it into view.

Jim would slip out of work early to cruise, lie to Herbert to bring off liaisons, and to his own dismay, he became a self-accusing sneak. He didn't like himself. He was emotionally faithful but just couldn't be so physically. Jim's carrying on wouldn't have been nearly as bad if Jim hadn't felt so damned guilty.

Many guilty people have a compelling need to share the responsibility, even to be found out, and to confess all to appalled and unwilling listeners. Eventually, they must spill the beans.

One night Herbert said to Jim, "You know, Jim, I not only love you more than anything in the world, but I also *like* you. You're the best friend I ever had." Jim was deeply touched at being so loved, and that was the last straw. He stormed into their bedroom and slammed the door. He fumed in there, then stomped back out to tell Herbert everything he'd been up to. Herbert didn't weep or rail or revile, but he did what was natural and appropriate. He threw up all over Jim.

Then each went to their mutual friends, each one of them explaining his side of things, and generally trying to enlist them into teams "for" and "against" the other, virtue versus the unseemly, the "Harmed Herberts" versus the "Randy Rover."

Of course, their friends had once starred in similar plots, so they clucked sympathetically and wondered what else was new. Among themselves, the friends predicted the two would both have new lovers before the year was out and were, sadly, proved right. The only problem was that Jim tended, in moments of passion, to call subsequent lovers "Herbert" and that proved less than endearing. Herbert made the same mistake until he learned to call them all "dear" or "darling."

They were still quite young when they parted, so neither had the perspective to know he had just lost the love of his life, the lover that would forever shadow all others. If either had known that he would never again feel such overwhelming passion, he might have felt profound loss or great relief, and he could have gone about his life with the calm that comes with knowing the worst and the best is over. As it was, each lived in the hope of duplicating the most passionately intense time of his life.

So all new lovers paled in comparison tests. Herbert would never find another man who could provide the Olympian satisfactions he had grown accustomed to with Jim, and Jim would never again love anyone enough to be as energized.

Herbert's company transferred him East to New York City, and he did very well in his job, despite some heavy drinking. Jim locked himself into a civil service job that promised the ultimate in care for the retiree and devoted his life to having "jam tomorrow."

Herbert and Jim became emotionally anchored in 1956, an Eisenhower year, before crow's-feet deepened to wrinkles, a little slackness in the gut blossomed into a barrel, and Dinah Shore was shouted off the charts by Madonna. Ever-briefer affairs were replaced by semi-regular sex partners, and clerks in stores started calling them "sir."

Jim came to admit that his cruising was now more habit than horniness. Although he was not given to fancy, when he went to tearooms now, he couldn't help but feel he was punching in at a job he had stayed at much too long. It didn't help that some of his old and regular tricks took to referring to his tool as "that old thing." He required increasingly baroque masturbatory fantasies and, when climax came, it was less Old Faithful and more molasses in January. Perhaps that explains why Jim raced to embrace old age eagerly when he turned a mere forty. He began dressing carelessly in loose clothes that revealed nothing, gave up diets, stopped dying his hair, and bought a cat with a disdainful nature. He made the emotional leap from forty to sixty in less than a year.

So Jim's years went by in a changeless way, a new year barely different from the old, until Jim finally retired and got "jam today."

Early on the morning of the day of his dreaded retirement lunch, he was shaving and feeling gloomy. He put down his razor and stared at his dick inquiringly, wincing at a bush that was now gray and a sharper reminder of age than any damned retirement lunch. He flopped his equipment over the edge of the sink, sucked in his gut to get a better view from above, and regarded his ornament balefully. He thought, *It looks like a drugged python,* then asked it, "What the hell have you ever done for me?" He waited and glared at it, as if he actually expected an answer. It just lolled on the sink, silent and unblinking.

"I've given you my life. I've sacrificed for you, devoted years to your happiness, given up love, lost Herbert, risked arrest, rolled about on filthy sheets, gone home with dangerous people, and suffered eight cases of crabs. So, tell me! Just, goddamn it, tell me: Were you worth it?"

This time his old friend stirred, and in his mind he was sure he heard a whispered *You bet your ass.*

Murder

It was too beautiful an autumn night to feel anything but serenely reassured that all was right with the world. The air was so pure, the massive clustered skyscrapers Dave saw to the west seemed close enough to touch.

Dave stood outside the Country Mouse, savoring the evening and waiting for Henry to come out of the restaurant. Henry had paused at the bar to speak to a friend.

Their dinner had been unsatisfactory. It had been weeks since Dave had been able to lure Henry out, and he had looked forward to their being together, to reassuring himself that their friendship remained sound. But Henry had been distracted throughout the meal, frequently checking his watch, paying little attention to what Dave said, often having to ask "What?" At one point during dinner Dave had asked Henry, "Are you due someplace?" Henry did not get the hint and simply said no.

In the many years they had known each other,

129

ROBERT C. REINHART

Dave Beldon and Henry Walkley had settled into a wholly unquestioning relationship; each allowed the other to be completely himself, whether the mood was sorrowful, soulful, exuberant, drunken, or droll. They exercised an undemanding tolerance that allowed them to say anything to each other. They could usually move easily into the most profound conversation. But not tonight.

They had survived being lovers, passed through the subsequent sense of betrayal that often follows, and had become even closer—deeply loving without the confusion of being lovers. So Dave shrugged off his dissatisfaction with the evening and left Henry to whatever distraction was making him such a clock-watcher.

Henry came out of the restaurant and said, "Why don't we take a cab?"

"What's the hurry?" Dave answered. "It's a beautiful night, and it's only twelve blocks to your corner. But if you're in a hurry—"

"No, I'm just being a twitch. I've no appointment. I wish I did. I wish I were rushing home to some incredible heap of meat and muscle."

They started down Third Avenue.

"Why don't you come to the baths with me?" Dave asked.

"Thanks anyway. I'll just go home and whack off."

"What gorgeous weather," said Dave. "No wonder I always get romantic in the fall. Most people feel their sap rising in the spring. Not me. It gets me in the fall. Every fall I get the urge to meet someone I can buy

The Prophet and Beatrix Potter figurines and stuffed animals for. Fall makes me foolish."

Henry was silent.

"There hasn't been anyone since Ben, has there?" Dave asked.

There was a slight pause before Henry answered. "No. I've had the funny feeling that Ben may have been the last, my last lover. He was everything I ever said I wanted and I couldn't stand it. He made me feel unworthy. Stop frowning, Dave. I know you didn't like him, but I did. I loved him. Still do...in a way. But not enough to do anything. You can be such a snob about people anyway. Much as I love you, I've never liked that in you. Still, I always haul my new lovers out to you for your approval."

"I never said a thing against Ben."

"Exactly. You were so incredibly polite to him."

"You liked him, and that's all I needed to know."

"I wonder where they all got to..." said Henry, "all those beautiful young men I loved. I tried to make a list of their names a few months ago. I couldn't even remember them all. Some had names, some faces, some bodies, some cocks—none had all the pieces. Well, a couple did. You were whole, of course. Ben was. But most were a bunch of bits and pieces."

Henry lapsed into silence and, searching for a reason for Henry's distracted behavior, Dave asked, "Are you having money troubles?"

"No, why?"

"Just wondered."

"I know what would make me feel wonderful.

Don't go to the baths, Dave. Come home with me. Come home and go to bed with me. Just for the hell of it."

Dave winced. "What a terrible idea. We'd either get the giggles or ruin a perfectly good friendship. Besides, you're too old for me."

"I'm only ten months older."

"Whatever put that idea into your head?"

"I remember our first time in bed," said Henry. "You're glowering, Dave. It's not an indecent memory. It was fun with you. We even laughed. I don't laugh much anymore. Not at all, come to think of it. How can I laugh when I'm concentrating on sucking in my stomach? I can't hold my breath and laugh at the same time."

Abruptly, Henry's attention was jerked toward a tall man in jeans on the opposite side of the street, and he stopped to watch, staring to confirm the man's identity. He watched with rigid concentration, a gloss of yearning on his face.

Dave thought he now knew what was bothering Henry: He was in love again. But the man across the street was not the one, because Henry looked disappointed.

Henry turned to see Dave staring at him and felt fearful that he had revealed his secret. He hoarded this secret like a child. To avoid possible questions, Henry said, "Now, that's my type."

They continued slowly down the cool street, talking of friends and work. Dave stopped with Henry at his corner to say good night, and Henry said, "Now, if I were in the Village I could kiss you good night," and he took Dave's hand and held it. He said, "Thank you for getting me out of the house. It was good for me. I'll be better company next time. I'll tell you what's been going on when I know myself. You're a lovely friend. You wear well. Don't get embarrassed. You're special to me. Now, go do something scandalous at the baths."

Dave watched Henry walk swiftly toward his apartment, then continued south, trying to shake off the faint discomfort. He wondered if Henry had become sentimental just to tease him. Dave was a man completely without intuition; it would have taken a subtler person than he was to see Henry's troubles.

Dave was sated but still lingered at the baths. He would finish his cigarette and then go home. Friday was the one night he permitted himself to stay out late. His work required him to be alert, so six nights per week he lived within strict limits, moderated his drinking, and was in bed by eleven. Friday was his evening to be intemperate.

A man he saw reminded him of Henry, and he thought back on the evening and that strange moment when Henry had suggested they go home together. That wouldn't have done. Such things just weren't possible. Imagine going to bed with an ex-lover. He had never heard of such a thing—especially when so much time has passed.

Dave walked to his locker, dressed, collected his valuables, and went to the elevator. The baths were on a high floor of a midtown office building.

In the full light near the elevators, Dave appears a somewhat unusual sight. Blue jeans and plaid muslin shirts were the common costume. Dave's suit, on the other hand, was excellently tailored, three-buttoned, one-center-vented, pinstriped, and the very model of Wall Street attire.

He came out into the autumn night and strolled, still savoring the evening. Ahead of him was a spill of sulfurous light from an all-night diner and the dim gray-pink of streetlamps. It was 3:30, and the city was filled with unfamiliar calm, its few noises particularized by the quiet.

Dave's stoic elevator man took him to his floor. As he opened the door he heard his phone ringing. No one ever called him after eleven. He told friends that if he was home at that hour he was asleep or busy.

The phone clanged on as he raced to his bedroom, angering him with its shrillness. "Hello!" he answered. "Yes, this is Dave Beldon. Who is this? What about Henry Walkley? Of course I know him...I had dinner with him tonight." And then his waspishness was slapped away by harsh, heavy fact. "My God. Yes, I'll be right over. Your name again? "

While waiting for the elevator, he wondered with irrelevant dread what the elevator man would think of his going-out again at this hour.

Henry's apartment was four blocks away, and Dave arrived without being aware of the space between. He entered the hall and rang Henry's bell. The buzzer sounded immediately and Dave pushed his way in. At the second-floor landing, the Riegels—Helen and

Conrad—stood in their robes, their ears cocked toward the third floor. His hello startled them. Instead of returning his greeting, they looked afraid and darted into their apartment. Dave felt as if they had hit him. He and Henry had dined with the couple often and knew them well. He understood that he was already heir to one of the bequests of tragedy; he was shunned. He climbed on.

The door to Henry's apartment was open, and a tall, impassive man leaned against the jamb. He had small, alert eyes, a headland of jaw, short faded brown hair, and a tall broad frame. To Dave he looked like Hollywood's idea of the Tammany type or Irish prelate or what he was: "I'm Detective Madden."

Dave felt himself being sized up but couldn't discern Madden's conclusions.

"The body's still there. I'd like you to identify it."

Dave followed Madden into the bedroom and stared stonily at the chaos of the bed. Madden drew the bloodied sheet back to reveal Henry's face, and Dave nodded confirmation that the brutalized man was his friend. There was so much blood that the bed still glistened wetly in places, as if printed with immense red peonies.

"Oh, Jesus," Dave said and left the bedroom.

In the living room Madden asked, "Close friend?"

"Yes, I'm his executor." Dave wondered why he'd added that fact.

"When did you see him last?"

"I left him on his corner after dinner."

"Time?"

"About twelve?"

"Where'd you have dinner?"

"The Country Mouse."

"It gay?"

"Yes."

"Either of you known there?"

"Both of us."

"What time you leave there?"

"About 11:30."

"Walk or cab?"

"We walked. It's not far."

"You didn't come home with him?"

"No."

"Went right home?"

"No. I went to the baths."

"Which one?"

"The Retreat on East Forty-sixth."

"They know you?"

"Yes."

"What time'd you get there?"

"A little after twelve."

"When'd you leave?"

"Just before you called. Three. Three-thirty?"

"Where'd Walkley say he was going?"

"Home."

"No other plans? No dates?"

"Not that I know of. No. I think he would've mentioned it."

"Why?"

"We're old friends."

"He go to any of the neighborhood gay bars?"

"Not often."

"He had any trouble lately?"

"Like what?"

"Take the wrong person home, find himself getting rolled, strange phone calls, fights?"

"He's never been in any messes. He's not the kind. He seemed to miss all the usual problems."

The questions continued, and from them Dave deduced that his and Henry's evening would be dissected, timed, and put in chronological order. The truth of Dave's alibi would be verified.

Detective Madden didn't say he was finished questioning Dave but closed his notebook and turned to go back to the bedroom. Dave asked, "Could you answer a couple of questions for me?"

"Sure," Madden said, stopping and turning back.

"How did you know to call me?"

"The people downstairs—the Riegels—they said your were friends and you lived in the neighborhood. They didn't think he had any relatives in the city. They reported the ruckus but not until half an hour after things quieted down. They said it seemed too quiet. When we got here the door was open, so we didn't have to force entry. But I'll need keys to close up. There any around?"

"I'll give you mine. What...well, what did they do to him?"

"Throat, abdomen slashed. Sexual mutilation. The bathroom's spotless. Whoever did it didn't even wash up. He must have been a bloody mess when he left."

"Oh, I see," Dave said, but he didn't.

"We'll call the next of kin, if you'll tell us who."

"There's only his mother. His father's dead. I'll call her. What should I do about taking care of the body?"

"We've got to take it down to the morgue and autopsy to see if we can find out what he was killed with. The medical examiner isn't here yet. We'll be here until the photographer and the rest of the lab people get done. We'll take anything we might find that might have some bearing on the case. We'll take the sheets, see if there's more than one person's blood or semen. We'll voucher and hold on to what we take as evidence, till we've got a case and criminal."

"Will there be an inquest?"

"Not until we've got a case, and this is one of the irrational ones. Tough, unless they keep on killing or they've killed the same way before."

"You'll lock the apartment?" Dave asked.

"Seal it for a day or so, till we've gone over things thoroughly. A second look a day or so later is usually the best time to size up what might be useful. Address books, letters—that kind of thing."

"The body?" Dave almost choked on the word.

"Probably done with it sometime Monday. You call me at the twenty-fourth precinct after five, I'll tell you. You got any questions, you call me. I caught the case, so it'll be mine."

A short, very thin man came puffing into the room carrying a small black bag, saying, "Why do they always live on the top floor?"

"He's in here," Madden said, leading the medical examiner into the bedroom.

Dave was left standing in the middle of the living room, neither asked to stay nor told to leave. Before him was a mirrored wall, and he felt sick at the sight of himself. He felt ragged and flayed, and looked it. He dismissed thoughts of himself and concentrated on what the police might find in the apartment. Henry's collection of pornography was not important: It would tell the police no more than they knew. They would also find Henry's address book. He hoped that would help. The address book might involve almost everyone Dave and Henry knew. But Henry's journals were an unknown quantity, one of Henry's oldest privacies, although he assured friends there was nothing about them in them, nothing but what he called his "literary musings." There were already a substantial number of volumes when Dave and Henry first met, and Dave had watched their number grow over the years, filling almost a whole shelf in the living room. Henry made his daily entries in red leather-bound books he had crafted privately, crowding their unruled pages in his crabbed hand. Dave went to the bookshelf, took down the last volume on the far right and found it half complete, the entry dated months before. That wasn't like Henry. The journal should have been up-to-date, to yesterday at least. Henry was scrupulous about keeping them timely. Dave glanced back through the pages, finding every day prior to the last entry accounted for. He put the book back, puzzled and nagged by Henry's inconsistency. As he went to shove the book back, he noticed the edge of a blue-covered book stuck behind the red ones.

He knew that as Henry's literary executor he would feel obliged to review the journals, and the idea bothered him. As he had told Henry when the subject had come up, he knew nothing about such things. Henry had told him to hire an editor and said it was his published works that most concerned him. Dave put the red book back, shook off this disquieting thought, and stared around the familiar room.

All around him were the artifacts of his friend's life souvenirs from many trips abroad, from birthdays and Christmases. Dave recognized some gifts as being from him. On a low round table stood an array of photos of Henry and his friend.

One evening Dave and Henry had sat on each side of that table getting companionably drunk, and Henry had told Dave why he kept that particular group of photographs: "It's my autobiography, in a way. Here you see me at twenty-two. I'd started writing my first book and I went right out and had an author's picture taken. I ordered twelve prints. Once for each copy sold, as it turned out. Note the shoulders on the suit; they run right out of the frame. Just look at me: Talk about dewy. I look edible—-and fattening—as if I were made out of marzipan. And there you see me in my 1958-author mood. I rented the pipe for the picture. My odd expression is the result of my trying to thrust my jaw out. All authors have strong jawlines. And there's me and me Mum in the early sixties. As you see, we've cunningly arranged ourselves to hide the entire Colosseum behind us. I had three books out by then. And there you see me early-hippie. I had my first young lover. They were all young after him and I was being aggressively youthful. You remember the sixties? That's when my nice Italian barber became a hairstylist. But my bulb of a face is still there, after all these years. I always look out of focus. And my eyes look damp. If you touched my cheek you'd leave a fingerprint."

Dave had once said, "You have a young quality. You look vulnerable. That's what you don't like. I suppose you're almost too good-looking. You'd rather look intelligent. It's not your fault."

"What isn't?" Henry had asked.

Madden appeared at the door and Dave saw him in the mirror. He turned to Madden and said, "You might want to know...Henry's will is in the center drawer of that desk, if it's any use to you. I have a copy. Henry's address book is there too, if you need it. Should I stay?"

"Just one last thing. Would you take that address book and copy out names of people he knew best? We'll start with them. He may have seen or talked to someone after you left him."

Dave went to the desk, removed the address book, and set to work. His sense of unreality peaked as occasional laughter came from the bedroom. The medical examiner left and a man went to the kitchen, where Dave heard a kettle filled and cups rattled. Dave finished the list feeling like Judas Iscariot: He had "kissed" everyone close to Henry and himself.

Madden returned holding a cup of coffee and asked, "Finished?"

Dave handed him the list, suddenly aware that there wasn't one woman's name on it. He had even left out Henry's mother, Lisbeth.

Madden glanced down the list, saying, "We'll be in touch with them. You can tell them they'll be hearing from us, if you want."

Dave didn't. Just let it happen. He couldn't face telling anyone Henry was dead. Let the police.

"Anything else I can do?" Dave asked.

"No. Far as we can tell, nothing's been stolen. Money, jewelry, credit cards lying all over. It wasn't for profit."

Dave nodded. Madden walked off. Dave was starting down the stairs when two men with a stretcher rounded the bend on the landing below. He edged around them and away.

He was almost home when Lisbeth came back to mind. Dave decided to wait before calling her. Despite the melodrama he knew she'd act out, he felt her son's death would only give her currency for conversation and allow her to play her favored role of martyr at an even shriller pitch. There would be hell to pay with her over any delay, because he knew he didn't have the right not to tell her immediately. He knew also that he couldn't cope with her.

Dave stopped at Henry's corner and looked back at the building. *Come home to bed with me,* Dave remembered.

What a terrible idea, he had answered.

What if he had gone home with Henry? Would that horror on the bed not be there? Would Henry have been saved, or would they both be dead? Would the shape of his life have stayed untwisted? He hadn't gone home with Henry because he was afraid of losing a friend.

Dave shivered at the idea that he might have been in that room. His imagination shaped a gargantuan figure hurtling into the bedroom, a glinting steel instrument poised, a massive arm arcing down, blood cascading in torrents.

Dave tried to think of Henry at dinner and was upset that no vivid picture of his friend would come. How long had it been since Dave had really looked at him? Certainly, that face he had identified for the police was no more than a mute, contorted counterfeit. But now his mind could not get past that image to the living Henry.

He tried to remember Henry's career. Again the impressions were blurred. Henry wrote whatever interested him. By dint of application rather than great talent, he had produced several books that had sold consistently over a long period, ensuring a very decent income. There were several cookbooks and some college textbooks. The book of hamburger recipes had sold steadily for fourteen years.

What else was there to remember? Henry picked his nose when he didn't think anyone was looking. (Was that an unkind memory?) Henry didn't laugh, he barked. Henry was not special in any particular sense, but he felt essential to those to whom he gave his friendship. Henry was serially monogamous, having had a string of lovers to whom he was faithful.

Dave felt ashamed for not being able to summon up a *whole* Henry.

He found that he had been standing for some time in front of a dry cleaner's window, his eyes fixed on a poster that showed a woman staring in alarmed horror at a blood-red smear of ketchup on her dress. He winced and hurried on.

CLIFFORD

I had mixed feelings when Clifford called to invite me back to my hometown to see our old school torn down.

I said, "Our school was built the year we were born. If it's grown old and useless, what does that say about us?"

"Exactly what you think it does. Anyway, they won't turn us into parking lots when we go down."

"Are there fewer Catholics?"

"Fewer children. The town's fading."

I hadn't seen Clifford in a while, so a razing was as good an excuse as any.

I hung up and went to root out our old high school yearbook.

I leafed through a volume that should have raised a welter of feelings, but didn't. I saw pictures of myself and was reminded that I'd been a good-looking kid but one I barely remembered. The activities listed under my posed portrait might as well have been things I'd been told when I wasn't paying attention.

I looked at Clifford's portrait and was amused to find I had more memories of him than of myself.

Clifford was a vivid child. He had very pink skin, knobby joints, and red-orange home-cut hair. He always seemed to be either growing into or out of his hand-me-down clothes. His face reminded me of *Our Gang*'s Alfalfa but a brightly colored version, lavishly dashed with freckles that ranged from sepia to burnt sienna. In the usual run of drab grade-schoolers, he looked gaudy, while I was a short, pudgy blob with fair clear skin, brown hair, and blue eyes.

Clifford and I met in fifth grade. He arrived mid-term, a new boy transferred to the parochial school I attended, bringing the class's total to thirty-nine.

Clifford's father had died, and he'd moved with his mother and grandmother from a fairly good neighborhood to a very poor one only three blocks from where I lived. But those three blocks were reckoned an unbridgeable gulf by my neighbors because wops lived there, and polacks. My home was on a block that clung to its lower-middle-class status by its fingernails, but we were upward-striving Germans and Irish.

It was the Depression, an era of impending, or all too present, poverty. But I was a child with a home, food, clothes, and toys, and as long as there was money for my addiction to movies, the world was agreeable and, in dark theaters, even magical.

Like Clifford's father, mine was also dead, having died of drink on a three-day bender, and I lived with my furious mother and two restless, much older sisters, all of whom worked. My sisters were pretty and dated a lot, while my mother had a series of lovers she seemed to dislike.

I can't imagine why my mother spent the money to send me to a parochial school, as she never showed the slightest sign of being Catholic, whereas Clifford's mother was pious and wanted him to be where he could be taught his faith and shielded from sin.

I don't know what parochial schools are like now, but in the thirties they were run on a stern military model. The nuns hauled God and sin into all our lessons, and He was presented as a disciplinarian given to tantrums of floods, frogs, and boils.

Sex was harped on, giving the place an air of lasciviousness. Believing sex could be lurking anywhere, the nuns spread the spicy scent of it. Girls of all ages were warned off boys, boys off girls, and boys were constantly ordered to keep their hands out of their pockets. (Until erections set in, their furious attention to busy hands in pockets baffled me.) Being homosexual never did come up, perhaps for fear of revealing an intriguing sexual novelty. Still, we knew something about it from grade school on because the boys giggled over stories of priests fondling boys and some older boys swore they'd been "touched up." It seemed to be accepted that priests prowled but, oddly, I never heard a priest called "fag," "queer," or "pansy."

It was within this spiritual hothouse that Clifford and I became friends.

I don't remember our first meeting, just that we were almost always together within days of his coming to my school. It seems odd to say that it was probably our gayness that drew us together. How gay can one be in fifth grade? That is, where were the words and experiences that would define us as gay a few years later? But I can look back now and know we responded to some affinity, some sensitivity to a shared specialness.

One hint should have been that neither Clifford nor I was considered a "real boy." Adults said this of both of us, and we both heard them. It was said in whispered asides we weren't supposed to hear and yet were meant to. Our classmates confirmed their parents' judgment of our boyish lack and were wary of us. Clifford and I were maladroit at sports, good students, and rather quiet. Also, neither of us could spit accurately or fart and belch on cue, much-admired talents of real boys.

We were canny enough to know that we should hide our deepest interests and share them only with each other. My darkest secrets were adult movies, books beyond my years, a passion to be a movie star, and revealing pictures of men, especially Hogarth's full-page Sunday comic strip of a near-naked Tarzan. For Clifford, they were drawing the costumes of movie heroines and cutting pictures of movie stars from the fan magazines he hoarded in cigar boxes. His drawings were precocious. No sticklike arms or childishly doodled hair for Clifford; his figures had solidity.

Clifford and I also shared a gift for being underfoot. No matter where we were in Clifford's home, that was where his mother said she needed to be. His home was a warren of small rooms that staggered about without any sense of order. The kitchen and an adjoining room that was too small for a bed were both used as sewing rooms for their alteration work, as they gabbled loudly in Polish, the grandmother's voice a querulous whine, the mother's a resigned drone.

I never felt welcome there, but neither did Clifford.

My mother was more direct in her prohibitions, and I was not allowed to have friends in when she wasn't home, nor were my sisters. Our mother treated us like boarders who were always late with the rent, and we were the targets of much exasperated sighing.

So Clifford and I were wanderers. We roamed the aisles of stores like finicky shoplifters, our favorite store being the new Woolworth's, the town's only air-conditioned store and a summer favorite. We walked and talked about many things, in all seasons and weathers, but mostly about movies.

We saw a lot of movies. I paid for mine by my irritating my mother and sisters into handing me change to get the hell out of the house. Clifford paid his way by spending hours accumulating bottles for their two-cent deposits.

We'd hunker down in the theater for hours, watching double features (and "extra added attractions") over and over.

While our classmates thrilled to Tom Mix kissing his horse, we doted on Bette Davis in *Dark Victory* and

Jezebel or Barbara Stanwyck being tough and sexy. Oh, to be loved while going blind or mad to Max Steiner music. Clifford was most taken with Marlene Dietrich and Carole Lombard and MGM movies because he thought they had the best costumes. I liked large gestures, melodrama, and stylish suffering. He liked sophisticated movies in which the heroine has a new costume for every scene. We wallowed happily in the delusion that movies showed a real world.

Movies held another fascination for me. When I'd go to pee in the middle of the movie, there would often be two or three men in the men's room. My appearance would fluster them and I would sense that I'd interrupted something. Or sometimes I'd go in and there'd be a man at a urinal holding his erection, and even at twelve, the sight left me slightly dizzy and hot with excitement.

The only thing Clifford and I didn't share was being devoutly Catholic. He was a believer. He wore his scapulars, went to confession every Saturday, and took communion almost daily. He collected holy cards with pictures of saints whose eyes rolled skyward, making them look as if they were about to pass out. Every room in his home had a crucifix on the wall, and when there was distress in his home, hard-earned money was spent on votive candles to put in front of their statue of Jesus.

I would see Clifford every Sunday in church with his mother and grandmother in one of the back pews, sitting with the other Polish people who lived in the parish. I sat alone, having been pressed into service by my mother to go to church on her behalf. Her last words to me as I left for church were always "Say a prayer for me," and I would trudge off thinking, *Go say your own damned prayers.*

By the sixth grade I knew I lacked faith. In the ninth grade I learned I lacked guts.

In the ninth grade sex got a death grip on boys' crotches. They passed around crudely printed pornography and their jokes became exclusively about sex, while something inside me stood apart and could only observe because I had absolutely no idea why girls were supposed to excite me.

I didn't want to do anything to a girl. Why would I?

In these times when sexual knowingness is a given, it may be hard to imagine that gay people once had no information except that their sex was, literally, unspeakable. Gay people learned about themselves, sexually and emotionally, in haphazard, hit-and-miss ways laden with danger and weighted with disgust.

Still, despite my ignorance, it was my undefined sexuality that drove me from Clifford.

One day a guy in my class pulled me aside on an empty stairwell and said, "I see you with Clifford all the time."

"And?" I had no idea where he was going.

"You know he's 'that way,' don't you?"

I must have looked blank. *Which way?* I wondered, and he read my incomprehension.

"Oh, don't be dim. He's queer. You're hanging around with a queer. Everybody's talking. Some of the guys even think you might be doing it with him."

I was too panicked to speak, until an answer came to me: "His mother does work for mine. She does her sewing." Then, to further protect myself and completely betray my friend, I added something like, "I had no idea he was queer. Jeez, you never know, do you?"

The guy took my betrayal for truth and walked off, warning, "You should watch it with him."

I thought, "I will, *I will*," then turned and hurried to the boys' room, where I raced into a stall because fear had turned my bowels to water.

I edged away from Clifford. No explanation to him, just a widening chilly distance.

When he suggested a movie, I made lame excuses about being busy. If I saw him coming my way, I dodged. I avoided places I guessed he might be.

I missed him terribly, but I couldn't afford him.

Risking being labeled queer was beyond my ability or courage. To be one of a crowd I gave up the only person with whom I could be myself. Instead, I chose to twist myself into shapes I hoped others would find pleasing. I even took a girlfriend as my virginal hostage to normality.

I'd sometimes see Clifford on the street, toting clothing to and from his family's customers, but I never remember seeing him with anyone. I see only a solitary figure, but I'm probably dramatizing the memory or, perhaps, still feeling guilty.

The nuns saw Clifford differently. He went to seven o'clock mass every morning, where he was usually one of two altar boys. He never missed a novena or special prayer service. The nuns singled him out for praise in class, and he got A's on his Latin tests. They doted on him and were sure his apparent devotion and intelligence might well lead him to the priesthood. They saw his solitude not as the result of ostracism but as a sign of spirituality. Their approval put even more distance between Clifford and his classmates.

Unlike Clifford—and to keep the nuns off my back—I went through the motions of being devout.

Sexually I was a late bloomer, and it wasn't until tenth grade that sex began to obsess me and, unlike in Hollywood movies, it was not sensitive and nuanced, well-lit, and underscored with music: Sex was as subtle as a cat-o'-nine-tails. I ran around constantly wanting to stick it in something, but usually settling for my less-than-romantic right hand.

By accident I discovered the town's train station, and it was a grubby and scary introduction to what it could mean to be gay.

The station was a great stone pile that strained toward grandeur, and its men's room was the city's center of gay revelry.

The room was a vast echoing space with ten or so urinals and six stalls, all lit by a stingy ration of appropriately piss-colored electric light that oozed down from dirty globes twenty feet above.

It was best to cruise when trains were due to arrive or depart so that one could get lost in the milling crowd. It was also the time when plainclothes cops couldn't easily sort the amorous from the itinerant. At such times most of the urinals and booths were full. When the travelers left, there was a residue of men with seemingly gargantuan bladders and handwashers who might have been scrubbing up to perform surgery. These men glanced and glanced and glanced, their looks rarely settling until they felt sure there were no cops among them.

Inside the booths, each marble partition had a peephole drilled by some dedicated gay mason. Through these peepholes, eye met eye and erections were displayed like goods for sale. Calling card–size mirrors placed on the floor enabled further inspection of the goods. Men rarely left together but would meet outside the station for a final assessment before closing the deal.

The possibility of arrest charged the atmosphere, as there were occasional raids. The place was made spookier by the unnatural silence of so many men moving stealthily. The only sounds were of footsteps and running water resonating in the vast space. If an atmosphere can have a taste, its was brackish.

Looking back on that bleak place, the comings, goings, and stayings in that men's room were like a slow-motion ballet for spies.

It scared the hell out of me, but I'd go there when I felt overwhelmed with loneliness. It wasn't just sex that lured me; it was the desperate need of a kid when he felt like he was the only queer in the world.

Except for what couldn't be avoided in school, I

didn't actually speak to Clifford until his grandmother's wake when we were both seniors and a month from graduation. The nuns urged Clifford's classmates to attend the wake and, in a show of perverse unity, the class decided to boycott the wake of the queer's grandmother. But the girl I was dating had a good heart and said that someone from our class should go to the funeral parlor, so she pressed me into service. It was a meagerly attended affair where the mostly elderly crowd spoke Polish. Clifford sat with his mother and fingered his rosary, rapidly shifting the beads along. His mother's face was tragic, and Clifford's expression spoke of nothing. Dorothy and I went up to them and mumbled appropriate banalities. Clifford's mother looked up and nodded. He rose and shook my hand but said nothing. He gazed past me to where his grandmother lay exposed to view. Dorothy and I stood around for a respectful amount of time before fleeing.

Days later Clifford disappeared from school. Rumor said he'd taken his grandmother's place at her sewing machine.

A week after graduation I moved to New York, planning to begin studying acting at the Neighborhood Playhouse in September.

Leaving home scared me, but the idea of staying terrified me, and I ran for my life.

The main difference in my life in New York was that I could be gay—not completely or freely in those days, but vastly more so. Gays were still mostly an underground community, but at least the knot in my gut untied. I could finally stop pretending to be a "real boy."

At the Playhouse I learned to handle a prop, fence, walk gracefully, negotiate iambic pentameter, and have wonderful sex. In New York my partners didn't look guilty, zip up, and run when it was over; they lingered, smoked, and talked.

Gays and straights commingled at the Playhouse. What counted was talent, and I had it. My acting teachers agreed that I had promise, and agents agreed that I was too tall, too thin, and absolutely impossible to cast.

So after two years of study and looking for acting jobs, I returned home to assess where I stood and where I might go. My mother took me in with moderate enthusiasm and repeatedly told me it was time for me to grow up and give up this acting nonsense. I should find a nice girl, get married, and settle down, a process that sounded like death in three acts. I got a job in a menswear store to put aside money and found other ways to stay out of the house while I plotted my second escape.

I heard the local dramatic society was casting *Detective Story* and went to audition, being cast as the young man who's arrested, a small, showy part. We'd rehearse four nights a week and weekends; I'd barely see my family. One day after my scene was rehearsed I was sent to have the show's costumer help me find something appropriate from their stock wardrobe. Their costumer was Clifford.

We looked at each other for a long time.

I was grateful when Clifford said, "Let's see if we have something right for your part."

We rummaged through the available clothes but found nothing that suited the character. Other players were now coming down to look for costumes, so I said, "Why don't I buy you a drink later and we can talk about how to dress the character."

"Coffee," he answered.

Over coffee I did most of the talking, being full of my worldly experiences and myself. After all, I now knew what martinis tasted like, I could order French food with fairly predictable results, and I'd been in an honest-to-God penthouse.

Clifford meted out his own recent biography. He and his mother now had a fairly successful business and still lived in the same house. He did some original work, designing dresses for weddings and costumes for the drama club.

The matter of us being gay didn't come up, and I might have thought Clifford was just one of those sexless people one hears of until I heard stories while in bed with fellow cast members. Clifford cruised the local train station and had been arrested about a year ago in a raid on the place. The story was that charges were dropped against everyone when it was found that one of those swept up in the raid was the mayor's nephew.

Clifford and I got in the habit of going for coffee after the show and then taking the same bus home. When I'd suggest we join others in the company for a bite after rehearsals, he'd look uncomfortable, so I'd say "Why don't we just do our usual," and he'd relax.

I rediscovered how pleasant it was to be with him. I found he had a shrewd, irreverent sense of humor. He was funny and smart, and I thought it a shame that others in the company might never get to know him.

We were together so often that I heard from some-one in the cast that everyone assumed we were lovers. This time I didn't care what they thought but, oddly, the idea puzzled me, because I'd never thought of him sexually.

When we were close to opening *Detective Story* Clifford brought in his costume designs for the prin-cipals of their next show, *The Women*. It was the kind of show in which the women's costumes were intend-ed to bring gasps of pleasure from the women in the audience. Clifford's costumes would. I raved to Clifford about them and he irritated me by turning away and shaking his head no, denying his talent.

By the time *Detective Story* was in performance, I'd saved the bare minimum for fleeing back to New York. I found a furnished room and began a round of theater jobs that would eventually lead me to work as a stage manager for Broadway shows and road companies. I loved the work, but mostly I loved the people I worked with. I wrote and called Clifford, who got a kick out of my theater stories and gossip. I urged him to come to New York for a visit, but he was always too busy.

I'd been back in New York about five years when I ran into a man I'd acted with in *Detective Story*. It was Saturday night at Shaw's Bar and very noisy. He was full of gossip about the town's theater group. I could barely hear him in the din or put faces to the names he mentioned, so I wasn't paying much attention until I heard Clifford's name.

He said, "It's just awful about Clifford, isn't it?"

"What's awful?"

"The beating."

"What beating?"

"A couple of months ago. Some guy lured him out of the train station, and when they got outside two goons showed up and beat him senseless. He was in the hospital for over a week. Lost most of the hearing in one ear. I thought he'd have told you, you two being so close and all."

It was sad to know that I was probably the last person he would have told.

I asked if they'd caught the guys who did it, and knew it was a dumb question. Clifford would never lodge a complaint and tell the town he was gay. Besides, the cops would do nothing, thinking he'd gotten what any fag deserved.

I'd developed a neurotic belief that, if I dared go back, I'd never be able to get out again, so I hadn't been back in two years. But I braced to go, because I got it into my head that Clifford needed rescuing. I was fired by indignation at what had been done to him and determined to make him face facts.

I called Clifford, asked him to book me a room at a local hotel and to have dinner with me.

A couple of days later, over dinner, I examined him, looking for signs of the beating. All I noticed was that he inclined his left ear toward me when I talked, so I assumed his right had been damaged.

Over coffee I said, "I'm gay." Clifford looked amused and shrugged.

I had to laugh. I said, "I've no idea why I thought you'd be surprised."

"Why tell me now?"

"Because I heard about your beating."

Clifford winced.

"You'd never have told me, would you?"

"What good would it do? It's past. I'm well. I can't undo it."

"But you can stop being a target," I said and began to lay out my grand scheme for how he was to live the rest of his life: He would leave this dreary burg and begin to hone his talents at the Fashion Institute. I'd get a daybed and he could sleep in my living room. I'd pick up some design or sewing work for him. I went on and on with the speech I'd rehearsed, never pausing to hear what Clifford might have to say. I finished with my clinching argument: "Being gay in this joint is like having a bounty on your head. Being gay can get you killed. Even the cops are your enemies. But more than that, in New York you could use your talents. You've got to get out of here."

Clifford looked at his drink for so long that I wanted to reach over and shake him. Dear sweet Jesus, didn't he hear me? Didn't he understand?

He asked, "How many times have you asked me to come visit?"

"Often. Dozens."

"Have you any idea how overwhelming that sounds to me? If I was too afraid to visit, how do you think I could live there? I can be scared enough here. I didn't tell you about the beating because I was ashamed, because I've always wanted you to think well of me, to respect me. I didn't like the idea that you'd think of me as a victim."

"How can you blame yourself for what those thugs did to you?"

"I don't blame myself, I just feel ashamed."

"So you'll turn the other cheek?"

"I don't think the beating was God's judgment on me. I was easy pickings for three thugs who wanted to prove they were men. I know how risky the train station is, that I shouldn't go there. I confess it and promise God I'll stay away, but I still go, even now.

"I pray to stop and I can't, so I accept what goes with it."

"You certainly don't think you deserve punishment?"

It took him a long time to say, "I don't know."

"Well, I do. You're too Catholic for your own good."

"I know you don't believe. And I probably believe more than I should. But I do have faith. I need it."

I said, "It could get you killed."

For the first time he looked angry, and said, "You don't know what you're talking about. It saved me."

"From what?"

"From suicide. Back in high school I knew I wasn't liked, but I wanted to graduate. Instead, my grandmother died and my mother was a month behind in the rent and two weeks behind in work. And there were all those doctor bills. She said it was either not graduate or get thrown out on the street. You know there's not much fight in me, so I did what I was told; I sat down at my grandmother's machine and learned to do the work." He looked past me at something painful. "That was as low as I ever hope to get. I worked, and all I thought of was committing suicide. I'd taken the barbiturates they gave my grandmother and hid them. It would only take twenty and I had forty. If that machine was all there was ahead of me, why live? That's what despair is: No past, no future—only some deadly present.

"The worst of it was that I couldn't tell anyone. I couldn't even confess it to a priest. I just woke up every morning and heard my mother already working, and I'd lie there and wonder whether I'd do it that day, take the pills."

Clifford lifted his glass of water.

"I'd always imagined that suicide would feel dramatic, full of turmoil. But it didn't. It just felt matter-of-fact, like just another minor chore. My problem was that I couldn't get past the idea that suicide would condemn my soul for eternity, that I'd just go from one hell to another. That's what kept me from doing it. So, no matter what you think, faith kept me going.

"Eventually the pain passed and I started to think about what I could do with what I had. I even started to think of doing some of the things I'd always wanted to do. And, bit by bit, it's happening.

"I know I have talent, but I don't have the courage

to leave here or to leave my mother on her own. I'm not like you, and you shouldn't expect me to be. I fit here, so I belong here. It's all I can handle."

You'd think that what he'd said would have shut me up. Not for a minute. He made sense, but so what? I'd written a script and rehearsed my lines and couldn't seem to stop myself.

I told him that he underestimated himself. I'd see him through.

I said more in the same vein, and he let me run on until I ran down. Then he reached across the table, put his hand over mine, and said, "It means a lot to know you care about what happens to me. I'm grateful."

I didn't want his gratitude.

I went back to New York with a load of anger at his mother, the guys who'd beaten him, the injustice of it all, and at Clifford for being such a patsy, and for wasting his talent.

We didn't speak again until I got tired of being righteous and called him. He said that his mother had been diagnosed with breast cancer.

I felt sorry for him. And furious.

For the next many years, my trips to my hometown were to avoid feeling guilty. I went back when my mother died and a little more than a year later, when Clifford's mother died. I went back to help Clifford move to his new home on a very pretty street. The ground floor would house his showroom and workrooms, and he'd live upstairs. I also went back for Clifford's thirtieth birthday, then his fortieth and fiftieth.

163

Every time I went back I noticed more buildings were down, more needed painting, more stores were for rent, and there were fewer people or cars.

Over the years Clifford had two lovers I knew of. I met one of them when he came to New York and Clifford asked me to show him around. He was certainly beautiful but a snobbish twit. His favorite phrase seemed to be "I wouldn't let my maid do that," and he spoke in an affected accent that was rather like a New York cop playing Henry Higgins. But I called Clifford and gave one of my better performances, saying that I liked the guy and hoped he made Clifford happy.

The second lover was a well-kept secret, as the man was married and, I somehow inferred, in politics. I never met him, never even knew his name. It lasted for years and ended when the man died suddenly.

Clifford was weeping when he called me and spoke between gasping sobs that hurt to hear. He said, "My friend is in the hospital. He's dying. His family is there day and night, so I can't see him. I never thought of that. I mean, I never thought beyond the times we could be together. And now..."

He trailed off, his "and now..." weighty with the fact that Clifford was now an unacknowledged and shameful secret, ostracized from his lover's life. He'd loved someone for years and now he'd become some dirty secret.

I said, "I'll come up," and Clifford said, "No, no! Please don't." For some reason, my suggestion alarmed him, and I said, "Of course I won't, if you don't want me to."

"I don't know if I can go to the wake or the funeral."

"I don't understand."

"Would my friend want me to?"

"You should. If it won't be too hard on you, you should. I'm sure he'd want you there," I said, doubting that was true.

Then Clifford started saying "I can't talk" over and over, but he didn't hang up, so I sat listening to his crying and silences and feeling useless.

The impact of what had happened to Clifford was clear when I visited him some months later and saw how much weight he'd lost. I asked him if he'd gone to the funeral and he said he hadn't, that it wouldn't have been right. Instead he'd paid to have a novena said and paid for his friend to be remembered at daily mass for a year.

He'd done what he could.

As to my own lovers, they wafted in and out of my life, until I came to understand I had almost no talent for being anyone's lover.

I was also late in noticing that I'd used up most of my future. Gray crept up from my beard to my head. I was seldom cruised and then, in what seemed only a few days later, never.

Our old school was only three stories high, so the tall crane with its wrecking ball would easily do the job. Clifford and I stayed well back to avoid the dust storm. Burly men with sledgehammers leaned against a truck. I looked up at the school's windows and tried to remember which classroom had been where and what the nuns' names had been. A fairly large crowd gathered, but there didn't seem to be anyone from our old class among them. Still, how likely was it that I'd recognize anyone after fifty years?

The crane growled to life and lifted the huge steel ball skyward, then swung it in a kind of backhanded slap, knocking away the corner of the school. Little by little, a place I knew I'd never escape became rubble.

I asked Clifford how he'd felt watching the school go down, and he said, "It wasn't the school I thought about, it was how intensely I'd felt everything and how confusing and painful most of it was. Now I wonder what all the fuss was about."

"For me, the fuss was about being gay and feeling that my life depended on keeping my secret."

We went to a mall for lunch, then wandered as aimlessly as any of the teenagers we saw. I tried to imagine that I'd ever looked that downy and failed. Was my face ever such a clear page? Were any of these kids gay? Was life easier for them than it had been for us?

That night we had an early meal and drove to a video store to rent a movie. In the "classics" section we found *The Letter*.

Near the movie's end Bette Davis shatters her husband by declaring "I still love the man I killed," and then wanders through a garden deep in shadow and lush music to be murdered by the wife of the lover she'd shot in the first reel. Then THE END zoomed out on a symphonic flourish.

Clifford sighed with satisfaction, and I said, "Better than fudge."

For that moment, I felt ten years old again and grateful that I still had my playmate.

RICHARD'S WINDOW

The young man was stunning. He was narrow in the hips and smooth as cream, with a washboard stomach and a swimmer's body. Richard could imagine those legs flicking like scissors as they barely churned the water, and he sped along to the music in Richard's mind—probably Vivaldi, maybe Strauss—and his arms drove the water behind him and thrust him like a missile meters ahead of his less skillful and less lithe competitors. Richard saw the swimmer's wet head shoot triumphantly up at the finish as the crowd cheered the most beautiful winner ever.

Richard shook the image out of his mind. But a swimmer was exactly the right image. Just look at his grace as he moved about his bedroom trying on shirts. Ah, the practiced smoothness of him as he held up the purple silk shirt, then threw it with such a fluid gesture onto the bed, then dipped sinuously to pluck the green shirt from the floor.

But what did the boy's occupation matter? He was stunning, the hero of some simple nineteenth-century rural romance or the model in the toothpaste ad with perfect occlusion or the boy in the Speedo ad whose breath would be like a breeze quivering through alfalfa.

Richard's shoulders were very tired and he felt faintly feverish and achy in the joints, the way he did in the hours before he came down with one of his killer colds. How long had he been standing at his window with arms raised as he followed the young man's activities through a set of powerful binoculars?

Richard threaded his way to the entrance of his darkened apartment, able to see fairly well from the light that spilled up from the street fourteen stories below. New York apartments are never completely dark.

He turned on the light in the foyer and just stood in a reverie over the young man. He'd been at his window for a long time and he was hungry, but he hated losing sight of the young man, even to eat. What was food compared to the delight of watching someone so unselfconsciously alone?

The truth was, in the week since the man had moved in and Richard had discovered him, he had rarely been alone. Richard was with him as the man poured Kellogg's Frosted Flakes and carefully sliced bananas into paper-thin discs at breakfast, and Richard joined him from the moment the man's light went on and Richard turned his off to take up his station by the window. Richard was amazed that the man couldn't feel his intense gaze. Richard always felt the connection his eyes made with the man, like radar encountering a solid and echoing it. He felt his sight and soul leaving his eyes and passing through the binoculars to rest on the man. How could the man not feel his hot look, not sense it as it stroked the pale hair on his arms, brushed against the nape of his neck, or slid gently over his lips?

The thought of the man was irresistible, and Richard turned off the foyer light again, went back to his window, picked up the binoculars from the sill and, arms stiff, resumed watching the man he had come to think of as "Bill," a simple, clean name that evoked no artifice, just a foursquare, unsullied personality without guile, without defects.

Richard had the man back in focus just as the man leaned over with large clippers to begin cutting his toenails. Richard put the binoculars down. He felt affronted. Perfect people didn't have to groom themselves. They were perfect without effort. Richard wished he hadn't seen his Bill do something so common.

By the end of the third week, Richard had conceived a biography for Bill. He knew all about him, his full name, family, his high school, and how popular he had been, and how bright and ambitious he must be. He knew Bill had come from his simple farming community to pursue a career in the arts and showed astonishing gifts in every area of dance, music, drama, and writing, as no single pursuit could begin to absorb Bill's stamina and remarkable talents. He also knew how in demand Bill was, and that was disturbing. So many were after Bill, both men and women, who sensed he was a rising star and wanted to attach themselves to him as he began his ascent. And

Richard was sure there were many who would use Bill, were even now urging Bill to sign lifelong contracts and seducing him with dinners at the best restaurants and evenings of riotous dancing at places only a select few were allowed into.

What really worried Richard was the cocaine and other drugs people were offering Bill so that they could have their way with him. Good God, didn't they know that they could destroy the very qualities in Bill they most wanted from him? It was just awful and would probably get worse if Richard didn't intervene, didn't come to Bill's rescue and show him how to lovingly nurture a career in ways that even the adulation of people all over the world couldn't corrupt.

Richard stepped back from the window and scolded himself for making up all this nonsense about the man; about Bill, that is—about Bill Wagner, to be exact. But he didn't scold himself too harshly. It was too wonderful to have Bill all to himself this way, to have his ideal made both flesh and fantasy.

By the end of his fourth week of watching he had given up all his other favorite windows and a cityscape that had once included the three pairs of male lovers in the high-rise on Fifty-fourth and a man and woman who were into rather baroque bondage in the building near the river. Now there was only Bill's window and only what Bill did that beguiled his eye and imagination. Other windows had claimed his interest and enthusiasm over the years as he upgraded to ever-stronger binoculars, but none had ever filled his mind and heart, or window, the way Bill did.

By the end of the fifth week of his relationship with Bill, Richard decided to take one step toward him. He knew the dangers of actually engaging reality, but what choice did he have?

On a Tuesday night Richard counted again to be sure Bill was on the twelfth floor and one apartment in from the left as Richard viewed it from the north. Richard left work early the next day and went to Bill's building, ringing bells randomly until some careless or lonely person buzzed him in. He walked to the second floor and, being careful to orient himself in respect to his own building, found that Bill lived in a D-line apartment. Richard returned to the bank of bells and found 12-D among the ninety-odd in the directory. So strong was Richard's biography of Bill that he was shocked that the name next to the bell was "C.A. Caspriel." Was Bill subletting from this Caspriel person? *No, of course not, silly,* Richard chided himself. Well, after weeks of knowing him as Bill Wagner, it did take some getting used to. Bill was really a C.A. (C. as in Charles? Carl? Carter? Christian? A. as in Arthur? Armand? Arnold? No, never Arnold.) and it wasn't Wagner but Caspriel. Not very musical, and how was it pronounced? Richard felt saddened. It was the first time Bill had disappointed him.

Richard went home and stationed himself at his window. The light soon went on in 12-D and, thank God, there was Bill Wagner. Richard felt so relieved to see Bill rather than that Caspriel person, he felt dizzy with relief.

Bill went out early and Richard sat in the dark getting very drunk, until he felt compelled to go down to Hustler's Row and bring home one of the young men who worked Fifty-third Street between Second and Third avenues. Richard felt unfaithful to Bill, but he was very lonely. The young man proved to be a cardboard consolation, but he would do for the night.

A few hours later Richard awoke to find the boy and odds and ends of jewelry gone. Nothing of much value, nothing more than he was used to losing, and he'd long since stopped buying anything he cared about having taken. He'd learned to factor certain losses into the price of these young men. But, unlike other times, Richard felt a certain poignancy about his life, because he knew he wouldn't drink as much or bring home unreliable people if he had Bill in his life. And he'd be so good for Bill. Richard would give Bill stability and security and encouragement. Richard would have a focus for his energy and his talent for management, and a constructive use for his money.

As soon as he got to his office next morning he called the investigation firm that vetted companies wanting credit from his organization. As assistant comptroller of Valutronics, Richard rarely dealt directly with Sidney Bell, the president of Corporate Assurances. This was different.

"Sidney, it's Richard over at Valutronics. I have a personal problem I thought you might be able to give me a hand with."

Since Valutronics was forty percent of Sidney Bell's business, he was eager with his offer to "do anything I can for you, Mr. Speers."

"A cousin of mine has just moved to New York," Richard said. "I barely know the young man. Seems nice enough. He's asked me to co-sign a loan for him. I know his mother fairly well. Actually, she's very close to my mother, but I don't know much about her son. Nice kid, but seems sort of vague about what he's doing for a living. Seems to have money enough to look after himself, but..." He let his note of doubt make its point by trailing off, then went on, "The loan isn't for a lot, but I thought I should know a bit more about him."

"The usual credit stuff?"

"That will be fine. Where he works, salary, debt, credit cards. Just the basics, Sidney," Richard said, using Bell's first name as a coaxing courtesy. "His name's C.A. Caspriel." Then, in a flash of inspiration, Richard went on, "Don't know his first name. Everybody always calls him C.A. Have since he was a baby. I suppose the C. is for Charles, like his father. But maybe not." Richard gave Bell the address and apartment number, then Bell asked, "Any rush?"

"I'm going to take him to lunch next Monday, so if you could have something for me by then."

"Get right on it," Bell said, then said, "This one's on us, Mr. Speers. Happy to have the chance to do you a favor."

"I really feel I should be billed, *Sidney*."

"Not on your life, Mr. Speers."

That night Richard felt closer to Bill than ever and was very disappointed when Bill came in, showered, put the clothes he'd been wearing back on, and went out.

Richard often wondered where he went every night, had even thought of following him, but knew he lacked the nerve. Richard was just grateful that Bill always came home alone. "Alone" left space for him and hope. As soon as he had Bell's report he would have the information he needed for a strategy of casual encounter in some bar or restaurant, in the lobby of the building where Bill worked or, even better, in the D'Agostino supermarket, where Richard might find out what Bill liked to eat so he could be sure he cooked the right things when Bill came to dinner.

Richard was at his office extra early on Monday morning, hoping that Sidney Bell would be eager to court his goodwill by being prompt with his report. Sure enough, Bell called when the clock read 9:01.

"Good morning, Sidney. You're early too, I see," Richard said and, trying for a casualness he didn't feel, added, "I always get my best work done early in the day. I suppose you're calling about that nephew of mine."

"Well, yes and no," Bell said and stopped Richard's heart. "The apartment at the address you gave me is leased to Caroline Althea Caspriel, but there's a guy living in it and the super doesn't know his name and none of the neighbors have met him. So, I'm not sure where I should go from here."

Richard was near tears and was afraid his feelings would leak into his voice. He covered the phone's mouthpiece and cleared his throat before he dared speak: "I'm afraid I've wasted your time by not being clearer, not getting all my facts straight."

"No trouble, Mr. Speers. I was looking forward to being of some help. I really appreciate your company's business, and we work hard to see that—"

"You always give us great service, Mr. Bell. We've never had anything but good results from the information you supply. I guess I'll just have to ask my mother about C.A. She'll want to know what he wants a loan for. She may even know. The loan's not for much, so maybe I'll just loan Bill the money."

"Bill?"

"I mean C.A. And, Mr. Bell, I insist that I pay for your services. Please. I insist."

Richard left his office early, stationed himself across the street from Bill's building at four, and waited until seven, when he gave up and trudged home.

He went immediately to his window but didn't pick up the binoculars, because Bill's window was still dark, the glass reflecting a piece of Richard's own building. Richard got a bottle of scotch and a glass and brought them to the window. The bottle was empty by 10:30 and Bill still wasn't home. That wasn't like Bill, and Richard was worried.

He set his alarm for midnight, rose, and went to find the window still dark. He set it again for two and rose to again find the window blank.

His three o'clock alarm woke him to an early hangover. He took two aspirin and went back to his station. His heart sped when he saw the window lit. He lifted his binoculars and saw that both rooms were lit but empty. He waited and ached with hope, then groaned when a lovely young blond woman came from the bathroom, her hands vigorously scrubbing a towel into her hair. He supposed she had a lovely body. She went back into the bathroom and came out again, tucking herself into a blue terry-cloth robe. She lifted a heavy suitcase onto the bed. Richard watched as she tossed clothes onto the spread.

Were she and his Bill going to live together? He couldn't bear the idea. But Bill wasn't there. Where was he? That hussy must be C.A. Whatever. What had she done with Bill? Turned him out? Ordered him into the street? Was he even now wandering homeless? It was too awful to think about. He couldn't think about it.

Richard put down the binoculars and dashed his knuckles at the tears on his cheeks, then went to fetch a fresh bottle of scotch.

Richard outraced a woman to the end of the checkout line and was enjoying his moment of triumph when he saw who was standing ahead of him.

He could actually feel his heart shudder when he saw the beautifully shaped head of sandy hair. Then the man glanced behind him and Richard felt terrified. It was Bill, his Bill. Bill who had run off without warning, and Bill who had enchanted his nights, and Bill who had been close and intimate for weeks and then had just disappeared. Well, he mustn't think of that. That was in the past, forgivable. All was forgivable now that he was back, looking so wonderful, so excitingly healthy. Then Bill brushed against him, his elbow skimming Richard's arm, leaving Richard feeling scorched and breathless.

Richard had never felt so at a loss for words or breath, so unable to act. His eyes dropped to the things Bill was placing on the checkout counter, and he thought, *Oh, Bill, you mustn't eat all those potato chips and drink all that soda. Dancers need stamina, good wholesome food. Swimmers can't be winners when they're full of saturated fats. Who's looking after you? What's happening with your painting and acting?*

Then Bill took his change and left, without so much as a glance back.

Richard paid for his three Stouffer's entrées and hurried out. Bill was nowhere in sight. Richard was breathless with loss. He couldn't believe it. Bill had been there, even brushed against him, seen him—no, not seen him, looked through him. How could Bill not sense, not know?

Richard walked down Fifty-seventh Street toward his building, trying not to be angry at himself. Was this just one of those lost opportunities life seemed so full of? His only consolation was that Bill might not be the person he had thought him to be.

But how much worse that loss would be if it weren't for that wonderfully lovely Donald who had just moved into 14-E in Bill's old building? To be sure, he was no Bill, but he was probably the kind that it took time to get to know. But Richard was already getting used to his habits.

After Norman: eulogy, memory, legacy

Eulogy

Hal didn't want to buy Louis lunch, so he discounted his obligation by choosing a moderately priced restaurant. He felt in some debt for the favor Louis had done him in helping him get a new client, but it didn't seem worth an expensive lunch. The client wasn't that good, and Hal had an acutely focused eye for social bookkeeping. He liked Louis well enough, the once or twice a year he saw him, but he never parted from Louis looking forward to their next meeting.

As they sat across from one another at Camille Chez Elle, he noticed that Louis was looking well. Not very happy but certainly well. The waiter came for their drink order. Louis asked for white wine and Hal for Perrier with a wedge of lime.

"Still not drinking, Hal?"

Hal gave the briefest shake of his head.

Louis put down his menu and said sadly, "I was rather hoping they'd have veal or English sole. I've been thinking of sole all morning." *Wouldn't he just,*

Hal thought, but said, "The salads here are always excellent."

"Oh, I never eat salads when it's this cool. What's good that's warm?"

"It's all fine," Hal said stiffly. "The food here is considered very fine."

"I've never heard of this place."

"I find it excellent," Hal said with more finality than he intended showing.

Louis looked aggrieved as he ordered a salad and handed the menu to the waiter with a sigh, as if he had just performed a mournful duty. Hal didn't care. He'd had a disagreeable morning in his office trying to help a client stay out of a jail he richly deserved for swindling his brokerage clients. He was squeezing this lunch in at a great cost in billable hours.

Louis made the gathering gloom even denser by saying, "Isn't it sad about Norman?"

"Everything's sad about Norman," Hal said testily.

Louis picked up Hal's use of the present tense and said, "Oh, dear! You don't know that Norman's dead. They found him three days ago."

Hal felt exposed and very resentful toward the several people who might have called to tell him about Norman. He thought bitterly that, even dead, Norman put him in the wrong, made him feel guilty.

"I didn't mean to spring it on you," Louis said. "Joel called me. He had to identify the body. Imagine! Joel's name was the only one the police could find in Norman's room."

Hal tried to dodge the subject by making a great

show of looking around for the waiter. He didn't want to know any more about Norman but worried that Louis might see a lack of inquisitiveness as revealing of hidden emotions he didn't feel and had no intention of simulating. So rather than avoid the subject, Hal decided that a tone of courteous curiosity would serve, turned back to Louis, and asked, "Did Joel say what he died of?"

"Fell in his room and cracked his head open. Bled to death. They think he was drunk."

Hal nodded. He wasn't surprised by the accident, just by how little he felt about the death of a man he had once believed he loved.

He couldn't bring himself to say he felt hurt that no one called to tell him, but he couldn't help saying, "I'm surprised Joel didn't call me."

"Maybe he wasn't sure he should. It's hard to know what's the right thing to do. Joel said he's Norman's executor."

Before he could modify the unkindness, Hal blurted, "Oh, Louis, can you imagine Norman having anything to leave anybody?"

Sadly, Louis couldn't, but he wouldn't confirm Hal's mean judgment by saying so. Instead, "Norman couldn't have been more than forty or so."

Hal thought for a moment and said, "Forty-two."

"Awfully young."

"He would have been forty-three in September."

Their salads came, and Louis looked at his as if some disagreeable surprise might be lurking under the lettuce.

Hal felt a rush of irritation and snapped, "For God's sake, Louis, if you don't want the damned salad, don't eat it. Order something else." Hal whipped around angrily in his chair to summon the waiter who, as usual, wasn't to be seen.

Louis looked hurt and Hal apologized. "I'm edgy, Louis. Bad morning. I'm sorry. I really want you to have something you'll enjoy. Please."

"I didn't mean to be the bearer of bad tidings. I know you and Norman were lovers. I just thought it was so long ago that—"

"It was. Too long ago to really matter. I haven't given Norman a thought in years," Hal said and switched subjects, saying too sincerely, "I mean it, Louis; if you don't feel like a salad, please have something else."

"You are upset about Norman."

"I'd be upset if I still felt much of anything about him." He lowered his voice and said reasonably, "I don't have one good memory of Norman, and that's sad. In a way, I wish I did."

Hal looked down at his own salad and found that it had turned nastily uninviting. Louis was right; the weather was too cool for salad.

Hal's last meeting with Norman had been bleak and, to this day, he was not sure what else he might have done to help Norman, although, as usual, he ended up feeling he should have done more.

He had last seen Norman after Norman came to his apartment from spending three nights sleeping on benches in Central Park. Or so Norman had told him when he called and asked to come by. Hal was never certain of the truth of anything Norman said and had never been sure whether Norman had an uncertain grip on reality, was a chronic liar, highly manipulative, or rampantly imaginative. Probably all those things. What Hal did notice that morning was that if Norman had spent three nights in the park, he looked surprisingly well and tidy for the experience. Norman's hair was as glossily blond as he remembered, if in need of cutting, and he looked wholesome and fresh, and preternaturally young. When Hal had opened the door to Norman, the sight of the man recalled a friend's remark about him: "Norman always looks clean enough to eat off."

Hal had wanted to ask Norman right off what he wanted and spare himself time and strained conversation, but he knew Norman would just look hurt if he didn't play his part in whatever fiction Norman had conceived. So Hal pretended that this was a spontaneous social call, and they dawdled over coffee and strangled small talk till Norman could edge toward his reason for coming.

Over a third cup of coffee, Norman told his tale. Hal found Norman's story disturbing and frightening, but Norman told it banteringly, making it sound as if he had chosen to have an amusing adventure, a lark. Norman illustrated his tale with quick, broad gestures, but Hal knew Norman kept his hands in flight to conceal the fact that they usually shook badly in the morning.

According to Norman, the man who was currently keeping him had tried to kill him in a drunken rage and then thrown him into the streets with only what he was wearing. Norman took this latest disruption in stride and thought that, since the weather was decent, he would rough it in the park till his lover came to his senses: "Just for the experience, you know. Just to see what it's like. You know, it's really not that bad, and I met some very interesting people." When he'd had enough "adventure," he had gone back to his love but found his way barred. The current lover was still upset and had gotten a court order to keep Norman from the building and even threatened legal action should Norman harass him. Norman was sure it was just a passing misunderstanding and would soon be put right. After all, they'd been together for two years and had had worse fights. Oh, and by the way, would Hal mind if he took a shower?

While Norman showered, Hal checked and found he had a little cash on hand, put two twenties aside to give Norman and, feeling devious, hid the rest.

Norman came out of the bath dressed and looking even more burnished. Norman tried to smile at Hal and failed, and then stood looking painfully lost, as if he'd reached too many unmarked roads. Hal turned away, and the twenties in his hand grew damp with sweat.

"I should be on my way," Norman said, but he lingered near the door till Hal pressed the money into his hand, then he brightened, smiled, and left without a word, only putting his hand lightly on Hal's shoulder to express affection or gratitude or something. Hal wasn't sure what.

Hal tried to follow Norman in his mind. Where would Norman go, or sleep, or shower, or get his next meal?

But as his concern grew, so did his bitterness. He'd had too many years of that man, and Norman, more than other disillusionments, made him realize how badly he chose lovers and how much he had always been willing to put up with just to maintain the self-deception that he wasn't alone. He would probably always resent Norman for giving him that insight into himself. Truth was, he had never been more alone than with Norman.

Hal walked into his bedroom, took his money out of hiding, and thought, *If Norman has nothing else to give, he certainly has the gift of guilt.*

Hal and Norman had begun their affair in adjoining urinals in a porno movie, eyes flashing interest, hearts pumping, hands grabbing. In his excitement Hal hauled Norman home, and it was almost two years till he could get him out.

Their first sex wasn't all that good, so they got drunk to give shape to the illusion that something splendid was happening between them. It took almost two quarts of vodka to arrive at bliss. Both were subject to the cheap magic of vodka in those days. What Hal didn't know for the first few days Norman lingered on was that Norman was at the porno movie because the sheriff had locked him out of his apartment that morning.

For the first few months after Norman moved in

they kept up the pretense that Norman was an artist, and Norman did have a portfolio of highly promising photographs and drawings to illustrate his claim. What Hal didn't know at the time was that the work had been done many years before and none since. Still, this slim body of work let them pretend. Hal made believe Norman would find himself, and Norman pretended he was looking.

Norman lived with Hal, but that implies that they were somehow connected in mind and spirit and body. Actually, they merely coexisted, living within sight of one another, their disaffections at a low but steady boil, Norman the more furtive antagonist for fear of being tossed out. The grievances Hal permitted himself to recognize were the small ones that hid his larger animosities and let him continue to see himself as the injured party in their disunion; Norman didn't rinse the sink after shaving, he jammed unfolded clothes into drawers, used the good silverware as hammers and screwdrivers, and worst of all, he drank too much, or more accurately, even more than Hal did.

But Norman had his uses. Norman's bad behavior greatly enhanced Hal's sense of superiority.

Booze and loneliness would occasionally spur them to inadequate, haphazard sex, always followed by a drunken argument.

The final rush to their bottom began over a table. They were getting ready to give a party, and at parties they could pretend easy affection for the invited audience.

The table was a gateleg antique, and in opening it

Norman forced the leg out under the leaf and broke it. Hal could hear the old wood snap, see the leg wobble in Norman's hand. Drink in hand, Hal yelled, "Jesus, Norman, you've broken it. You're a clumsy goddamned fool, and that's a very expensive antique."

Norman looked bewildered and said, "I didn't break it."

"What?"

"I didn't break it."

"For Christ's sake, I just saw you."

"I didn't do it," Norman said near tears.

And even through the blur of booze, Hal knew somehow that Norman really believed he hadn't, that in an instant Norman had obliterated a disturbing reality and made his innocence fact. In that moment Hal understood that if Norman believed he wasn't to blame, was able to erase responsibility, there was a great void that neither could ever hope to fill.

A week after that there was the suicide note.

Hal came in late from work to find Norman sprawled across the bed fully clothed. Norman faced away from him, and the minute Hal saw him, saw how inert he was, he felt breathless panic. Instinct and dread made Hal afraid to touch him. A scrawled note lay next to Norman on the sheet. Hal grabbed it and moved as far from the bed as he could. He was trembling, already fearing the police and tangled explanations.

The note began, "I have an intolerable sadness and hurt inside me. I can't do anything right, because there's no one to do it for, not even myself." How terrible! Hal began to weep just as Norman began to snore. He walked to the far side of the bed to look at Norman's face, and his foot hit an empty vodka bottle and sent it spinning.

The next day Hal told Norman he had a month to find somewhere else to live. Within two weeks Norman found Clarence and moved in with him.

Three years after Norman left Hal's home, Norman made his first foray back into Hal's life.

Hal came through his front door early one evening to the sound of his phone and answered to hear Norman ask, "Hal?"

Hal said warily, "How are you, Norman?"

"I'm fine, feeling really good."

They chatted like two weary people stranded in an airport lounge before Norman could bring himself to ask, "Would you mind doing me a favor?"

Hal became guarded and said with uneasy reserve, "If I can."

"Would you mind bringing me some cigarettes?"

Odd, Hal thought, and asked, "Where are you?"

"Well, I'm in Bellevue, but it's just some mistake."

Hal knew that if Norman said it was a mistake, for him it was, so he just said, "What kind of cigarettes do you want? When are visiting hours?"

Hal had difficulty finding the psychiatric wing in the sprawl of Bellevue's buildings, and when he did he entered a fortress. He had to sign in and walk through a metal detector, then wait in front of a large steel door while a guard phoned to someone inside that Norman Thompson had a visitor.

Norman was insistently charming, full of thanks for the cigarettes and of explanations for his mistaken presence among mentally disturbed people. They sat at an iron table and talked, Norman making clear that they had assigned him to this ward through some clerical error that he was assured would soon be put right. Since he was here, he was making himself useful to the staff in organizing the patients' time and amusements. He told Hal several times that Hal would be surprised to find what really nice people were here. Norman talked and Hal thought of the broken table. Like the table, for Norman this wasn't happening, wasn't at all what it seemed. Norman willed it different, so it was.

Norman smoked cigarette after cigarette, and Hal idly wondered how long the carton he brought would last. But even through the heavy fog of smoke around Norman came the biting odor of chemicals. Could one smell mind-leveling tranquilizers? But for all the Thorazine Hal guessed Norman was taking, Norman didn't seem much different to him: He still spoke brightly, smiled engagingly, waved his hands about, talked as if they had just run into one another at a party. As with most of his time with the man, Hal felt his sense of reality going askew and, under Norman's spell, was almost able to disperse the sad evidence of numbed patients and paper slippers, of shuffling feet and the solitary mumbling people who sat along the wall.

When Hal finally rose to go, Norman stood with him and thanked him courteously for his visit and

191

said how nice it was to see him again. Norman walked Hal toward the door to the ward and Hal paused a few feet from the guard to ask Norman if he was allowed to have money, a twenty already wadded in his hand.

Norman said, "It's kind of you to ask, but I'm sure they'll realize their mistake and then I can go about my business." Hal wondered what that business could be. He pressed the money into Norman's hand.

Norman started to walk toward the door with Hal, but the guard rose and looked a warning at Norman and Norman stopped, looking confused. Hal moved on, turning back when he was at the door. Without raising his hand from his side, Norman signaled a small, secretive goodbye with the slightest flutter of his fingers.

Hal would never forget the shuddering boom of that door thudding shut behind him. He would always think that if dread finality had a sound, it would be the daunting noise of that door closing Norman in.

"The desserts here are excellent, Louis. And, for God's sake, don't tell me you're on a diet."

"As a matter of fact, I am, but the hell with it."

They ordered. Hal sat and fidgeted, resenting Norman's ghost.

Hal asked, "Did Joel tell you much about what happened to Norman?"

"Not much to tell. He'd been living in some kind of welfare hotel after they let him out of that last detox. I ran into him a few months ago, and you wouldn't have known he had any problems at all. He looked terrific. You certainly wouldn't have believed he was over forty. The booze seemed to preserve him."

Hal laughed.

"I suppose that is funny," Louis allowed, taking a bite of the cake that was set before him and smiling benignly, looking as if he had bitten into bliss.

They parted outside the restaurant with the usual obligatory protestations that they would get together soon, that it had been too long since the last time, but neither lost any time in hurrying away as soon as decency allowed.

Norman's shadow walked back to Hal's office with him, stayed around all afternoon, lighting a rotten day with a baleful light.

Hal tried to exhume a happy memory of Norman and couldn't. Then he searched for some thought or word of kindness for Norman and for their time together. He couldn't find a benediction. The word that kept occurring to Hal was *sad*. But that seemed a small, bleak epitaph. Sad that Norman had barely left an empty space when he died. Sad that there had been only one name left for the police to call. He wanted Norman's ending to be more than merely sad, but that seemed to be all that was left, a life distilled to something as small and vague as that word.

If he had been a religious man he might have said a prayer for Norman. If he had been more caring or curious he might have called Joel and found out where Norman was buried and who tended to his last needs.

He barely remembered his years with Norman; only the brief encounters afterward were vivid. It was in those times that Norman seemed intense and real. Norman's death seemed neither. His death seemed as dismissively secretive as folded money pressed into an eager hand or the fleeting graze of Norman's hand on his shoulder that last morning that might have been taken to mean a great deal or nothing. It should have added up to more, but Norman's death seemed to have no more substance than his fingers fluttering in a goodbye the guard wasn't supposed to see.

Memory

"I hope to Christ it wasn't AIDS. It's been years, but still..."

Harley stopped speaking to motion the waiter over and take a glass of champagne from the silver tray. The waiter edged the tray toward Dominic, who gave a slight shake of his head.

Harley said, "Oh, have some more. It's excellent champagne. Only the best at my openings."

"I'm going on to Charlotte's for dinner. I'll need my wits about me."

"You certainly will. How is the old witch."

"Still rich, still buying my best porcelain."

"Shame she doesn't buy paintings," Harley said and glanced critically at the violently colored abstract paintings that crowded the walls of his gallery. "Bill's changed his palette, and I can't say I like it. His last show was half sold before the opening. So far, not a single sale out of this lot. I told him they were too damned forceful. People don't like to live around all that energy."

Harley tugged his eyes from the offending art, sighed and went on: "It certainly isn't my week." He summoned a bright smile and flickered his fingers at a woman in black crepe who stood across the room with a very untidy-looking man Harley didn't know.

He turned his back on her and said, "I should go talk to Heather. She's always *so-o-o* interested in the work. She talks it to death. Never buys a damned thing, but she knows everybody."

Dominic tried to sneak a look at his watch, but Harley caught his furtive gesture. Harley didn't want him to leave, because there was no one else to whom he could talk about Norman, no one else among his acquaintances who would even remember Norman.

"I can tell you that Norman's dying was the last thing I needed the morning of an opening. I wonder who paid for his obituary in the *Times*. They're very expensive. Nothing in it about how he died, or where, or if there'd be a service.

"When I saw Norman's name in the paper I actually jumped. Spilled coffee all over myself. If he'd had any sense he might still be alive.

"If he'd had the sense to stay with me he could have had anything from me, and he knew it. He certainly had everything he wanted when he was with me. I didn't ask much. I wasn't demanding. I never am. All I really insisted on with him was no drugs. I let Chris have his drugs. I didn't know any better then and, Lord knows, coke was common enough in my crowd.

But after what happened to Chris, I wasn't going to have that in my life again. You remember what happened with Chris: the police, his family, the IRS. Things were not going to be that way with Norman.

"I even paid for his courses at Parsons, but I don't think he went much. He'd say he was going to class and come home drunk. I could even shrug that off. After all, I had to be out almost every evening on business. Norman called them parties, but for me those evenings were business. He could never understand that eating and drinking is part of the way I make a living.

"Did you know he once had talent? He had this portfolio of his work. I was impressed, thought I might nurture it. But talent's never enough, not without drive. Seen too much of that in my time. Like dynamite without a fuse.

"When he was with me, I even talked to my lawyer about a trust fund for him. I never once asked him to go to work. He always had money in his pocket. I didn't want anything from him. My Lord, what did that poor boy have that I could want? His family certainly didn't have anything. Dirt-poor and rather awful, from what Norman said."

Harley waved over a passing waiter, placed his empty glass on the tray, and took a full one, saying, "My last."

He sipped and said, "But, Christ, he was so beautiful. One of the most beautiful men I've ever met. Everybody envied me. It's a character flaw, but I love being envied."

"Who doesn't?"

Harley shrugged and said in a flat tone that denied his assertion, "I love beautiful things." He sipped and again regarded the paintings sourly, saying, "I suppose that's why I hate these new pictures. They're assertive and strident. They demand attention.

"It wasn't my fault Norman left. I certainly never asked him to. Packed one little bag while I was at the gallery and was gone when I got home. Didn't hear from him for a year, then he called and asked if I could let him have a hundred. Why not?

"But no real regrets. He was never really there. One of those people who's half in the last place and half in the next but never where his body is. That make sense?"

"Do you suppose he kept his glorious looks?" Harley asked and answered himself, "Don't see how he could, with all that booze."

Dominic glanced openly at his watch.

"Mustn't keep Charlotte waiting, Dominic. She hates it when people are late. I made that mistake. Once! She was glacial all evening."

Dominic nodded. "Well, I'm sorry about Norman. Beautiful boy but a perfectly terrible lay. He was the only lover I was never jealous of. He hated sex. Still, if he'd fucked like he looked I would probably be dead."

Dominic laughed and said, "Must go."

"Say hello to Charlotte for me."

He watched Dominic walk toward the massive bronze art deco doors of his gallery and thought, *No, it couldn't have been AIDS. He hated sex.*

Harley walked toward Mrs. Belmer thinking that

197

he must remember to call Nicky and tell him he would be home to dinner even later than he'd imagined. Dear Nicky. Not at all like Norman. Thank God!

Legacy

The blue-green and gold illustrated universe vaulted over him, but for all its vast majesty, the near-empty Grand Central Terminal made him uneasy at 7:45 on a Saturday morning. Only an out-of-towner, someone without a New Yorker's sense of the sacredness of weekend mornings, would arrive at this hour—an out-of-towner and the homeless who were now regrouping.

He strolled toward Gate 12, and as he neared it he could hear the thud and hiss of a train grinding to a stop. Meg was easy to find among the thirty or so passengers chugging up the ramp toward him. She was a down pillow of a woman. He noticed that her hair was newly and too tightly permanent-waved. He smiled, remembering that women in his hometown got "perms" like Meg's, perms that *lasted* and were kept till only bits of curl crimped the ends of straight strands. Pinned to her hair was a neat flowered hat that owed nothing to any period or style. He smiled at her pale pink suit of some luminous synthetic fabric, which, knowing her as well as he did, she had probably bought just to wear "for special." His affection for her warmed his face as he grabbed her in a tight hug.

"Who-o-oph!" she went as he squeezed the breath out of her. "Careful, dear, you'll get my hat out of whack. And I'm not going into the Ladies in this place to put it right."

"You look terrific. C'mon, we'll get you some breakfast. You hungry?"

"Always. That's why I had to let this suit out before I could get into it."

He didn't know what might be open nearby at this hour, and after some scouting they settled for the McDonald's nearby on Forty-second Street, both ordering pancakes and sausages in the almost deserted restaurant.

Joel pushed the sticky syrup container away from himself and moved his coffee near, then reached in his shirt pocket and pulled out a clipping hardly bigger than a postage stamp. It was Norman's obituary from the *New York Times*.

"Here," he said, passing it to her. "I sent the copies, but I thought maybe you'd like to have the original."

She took it without looking at it and tucked it carefully into the bulging wallet she took from her crowded purse.

"You send me the bill for this now, you hear?" she said.

"I'll take care of it."

"It was my idea. I wanted it for him. He lived here most of his life. People knew him. Besides, he was family, my nephew."

"It was expensive."

"Please, Joel, you send it along."

He nodded to end the matter, knowing he wouldn't do as she asked.

"What time do we have to be there?" she asked.

"The city's paid the rent through today, so we've

199

got all day. I don't think there's much to do."

"Still, somebody should have a look. I'd like to get the three-twenty back, get home while it's still light. The station back home is scary after dark."

"More coffee?"

"Sure, and bring me one of those Danish I saw."

He came back with the coffee and pastry and put them in front of her. She pushed two dollars toward him and he said, "It's on me," and she said firmly, "No, it's not."

He left the money where it lay to signal his unwillingness and said, "Watch the pastry. It's hot," then asked, "How's Norman's mother?"

An angry look flashed across her face and she gestured sharply, as if swatting away a pesky fly.

"We haven't been speaking again. I suppose we'll make it up. Maybe not. I don't know if I want to this time, not after this.

"Damn her! This is like everything awful that's ever happened in that woman's life; pretends the catastrophe's not there, and if she does open her mouth about it, you wish she hadn't. And her own son. 'Now look what's happened,' she says. 'Just like his father.' Norman certainly wasn't like his mother. Norman knew how to have some fun. Not an ounce of fun in my sister. She should have gone ahead and been a nun like she wanted. If she hadn't gotten pregnant by Hal, she probably would have."

"I never knew."

"Nothing wrong in getting in the family way if she'd loved Hal. But she didn't, and she was too

Catholic for anybody's good. She still thinks God told her to marry a drunk and have the baby. And then have more. My sister never had an ounce of sense. She only knew what was moral and right, never knew what was best for herself or anybody else. I suppose it's all she knew, what she was raised to. But we had the same parents, so she's hard to figure." Meg sighed and flicked her hand, as if to shoo away the past.

"What's it matter? If she changed tomorrow it would be too late to do Norman any good. Dear Mother of Jesus, imagine having to be shamed into burying your own son. She didn't want him in the family plot. There's room for an army. The Sullivans own more acreage for the dead than they do for the living."

Her mouth closed to a taut line, as if to trap words better not spoken. "Oh, God, don't let me get started.

"Anything bad that happens in this family seems to bring up every awful mess we've ever been through. We get to fighting over stuff that happened fifty years ago and then it all gets jammed back down, and we go back to pretending nothing's happened and we're all just the happiest family that ever hit Haspen Street. You must know we weren't; you lived next door. You were Norman's best friend. He must have told you."

Joel nodded and said, "Mom always turned the radio up when they started. She said it wasn't nice to eavesdrop on people's troubles."

"You must have heard a lot of radio." She put the Danish to her lips gingerly, then put it back on the plate untasted. "Still too hot. How do they get them so hot? God, I feel crabby." She pushed the Danish away. "Oh, shit! Norman should have had better. A drunken father who beat up on everybody, a mother with too much religion and no gumption. And what could I do? They wouldn't have anything to do with me till my Frank died."

Joel was surprised. He'd never seen her angry, never heard her speak bitterly. She had always been Norman's favorite aunt and, by affection, his adopted one; the funny, nice lady who dispensed treats and laughed with them and gave them a place to hide out when they were children in disfavor with their families. And when Norman and he were older and moved to New York, she would come down and take them to lunch, even buy them a martini and then take them shopping at Macy's for a shirt or tie or something that seemed extra special because they could barely make the rent on the apartment they shared. She was their valued and loved friend. They told her the truth about their feelings because they knew they were safe with her. Later, she was the one they tried out their new lovers on and she was the one who approved of them all, even when they themselves weren't quite sure or had already decided that Tom was preferable to Dick who by then was about to be succeeded by Harry. And she had remained Norman's ally when everything went against him and he turned against himself. She was even faithful when he turned against her too.

"Well," she said, "it's all in the past. Tell me: How are you doing?"

"Same old job. Still Barnes & Noble. I like it there. Actually, I'm very happy there."

"How's Jerry?"

"Up home with his family. He said to give you his love."

"Why don't you ever bring him up home with you?"

"Oh, Meg, you know why. Mom knows, but she doesn't want to see any evidence of the crime."

"You may be wrong about her."

"I may be right."

They didn't linger in front of the once elegant Pierpont Hotel on Waverly Place, but hurried up the diseased stone steps in a lobby that commingled remnants of chipped pink marble and carved oak with distressed vinyl and chrome furniture. A reception desk was placed to provide a view of the waiting area and constructed more to ward off attack than to dispense hospitality.

Joel was happy to see that there was no one at the desk, because he wasn't sure what his legal rights were. The police had let him keep the key to the room, but did he need some kind of permit to take Norman's things away, even though he was the executor? They walked quickly to the elevator, and Joel pushed a button that wobbled in its socket. Above he heard a grinding noise as the elevator shuffled bumpily down.

The fourth-floor hallway was painted a sour apple–green, and the vinyl tiles that remained on the floor curved up at the corners like a surreal vision of the sea.

When they were in Norman's room, Meg leaned against the door and blessed herself in a rapid sweep from forehead to breastbone to shoulders, left, right. Then she began to weep. Joel touched her shoulder and she flinched. He tossed some shirts off the room's only chair and onto the bed so she could sit. He peered critically at the chair and retrieved one of the shirts to dust it. He helped Meg into the chair, sat on the bed, and put his hand over hers as she sat shaking her head. Such an awful place. It reeked of disinfectant and sour laundry.

The room had a mean-spirited air, and it seemed all too familiar from movies about down-and-outers and from TV news reports on SROs. The drapes were two skimpy strips of plastic with a leaf pattern printed in acid-green. The chair was no better than the cheapest garden furniture. The bed was only a mattress on a frame, a tattered spread covering it, a broad swatch of oily dirt on the wall at its head. The room was inhospitable, as if to discourage people lingering.

"Oh, Joel, isn't this an awful place. When I walked in, all I could see was that beautiful boy in this...this hole. I only have my retirement money, but I could have helped some. He shouldn't have had to end up here."

Joel pressed her hand.

"Oh, God. I'd love a glass of water, but not out of that," she said, indicating with a nod the tiny scarred and rust-stained sink in the corner.

"I'll go get us sodas."

"No, let's just finish and get out of here. There

can't be much. Where would he put it? Do we have to take his things away?"

"I don't know."

Neither moved, just stared about, as if trying to understand some great puzzle.

"My sister is a weak woman. Never stood up to that husband of hers. If she wanted to take his abuse, that was her business. But not to protect her children. If she believed God gave them to her, she didn't take very good care of His gift.

"Did you know my own sister didn't speak to me for fifteen years because of my Frank? I was judged and found wanting. My Frank was Catholic, and his wife wouldn't divorce him. So we lived together. My own sister called me a whore and said she wouldn't have my kind of woman anywhere near her family. Norman was only two when Frank died, so Norman never knew any of this. Too awful for decent folks to talk about.

"We patched it up after Frank died. Lord knows, I needed someone. I had no idea anybody could feel as alone as I did. Well, isn't that what families are for? For comfort. But I found out she told our sister Cecelia—God rest her soul—that Frank's death was God's judgment because we'd been living in sin. Thank Christ she never said that to me. How could I have ever spoken to her again?

"I never told Norman about Frank and me, about my troubles with his mother. It might have helped him to know I had my troubles with his mother too. But who knows?

"My sister never gave a damn whether anybody was happy. She always believed they had to be up to something pretty awful if they were.

"That's what got to her about Norman. He seemed happy. I think it was that more than his being gay that got up her nose. Do you know what she said to me? 'My son is dead,' and that was that for her. She could dispense with whole lives with one of her superior sniffs and a rosary or two. She didn't want him in her life, but I did."

"He loved you," Joel said.

"Oh, no, Joel. After she threw him out he didn't want to have anything to do with any of us. I was one of *them*. I couldn't blame him. We'd never been very good for him. I just hoped it saved him pain to be away from the lot of us.

"Norman only called when he absolutely had to. I knew how much he must need help to turn to anyone in the family, even me. And I always felt awful to think of his needing help and bad about giving it. Giving people money never makes a friend. It hurts to ask, and it's awful to owe."

Joel had never heard her like this, and it unsettled him. He ached to see her so low and to see her take so much on herself. "It wasn't just you," he said. "It got so he didn't want me around either, not when things were really bad. He evaded me, and when we did get together it was uncomfortable. I pretty much gave up. What can you do when someone keeps pushing you away?"

She sighed and struggled from the chair. "Let's finish up and go get some lunch. And a good stiff drink."

Joel emptied the contents of the small, shallow closet onto the bed and put the large black artist's portfolio on the floor. Meg lifted each piece of clothing and made a neat pile of very little. He took some underclothes and shirts from the tiny, rickety chest of drawers and gave them to her to sort. Joel peered under the bed, saw two empty liquor bottles, stood, brushed his knees clean, and said nothing. They sorted through the few out-of-fashion clothes and flimsy drip-dry shirts, concluding there was nothing worth taking away. Joel dumped the few toiletries on the glass shelf over the sink into the rusted wastebasket below.

He regarded the orderly pile of clothes on the bed and asked, "Salvation Army?"

"Doesn't seem to be much they could use." He nodded.

She gestured toward the portfolio and asked, "You know what's in there?"

"Yes."

She cocked her head in question.

He said, "His old drawings and photos. From when he was at Parsons. I'll take them with me."

"I'd like to see."

He looked embarrassed and said, "They're all male nudes."

She laughed and stopped, then started to laugh harder, finally gasping out, "You protecting my pure old soul, dear? Old ladies shouldn't look?" He dipped his head to hide his discomfort. Sparing her a sight she might find sordid was certainly one of his reasons. She smiled: Joel had always blushed at teasing or a compliment. She said, "C'mon, let's see."

He looked as self-conscious as a novice shoplifter but undid the string ties on the sides of the portfolio and set it on the bed.

He hadn't seen these pictures in years, but remembered them as erotic and beautiful, but that was years ago, when he was young and his taste in art unformed. He'd hate to see them now as just shoddy or inept or just clumsy porn.

Meg flipped the folder open, and on top was a photograph of a man of twenty or so with a swimmer's body, muscles carved in long, smoothly tapering mounds. The man lay on his side, gazing squarely at the camera; an amused, insolent look on his face, his cock not quite hard. Even reclining, even in black-and-white, the man looked swift and vital and about to say something impudent that would make you laugh.

"What a lovely man," Meg said. "Haven't seen anything like him since I was a girl." She glanced over to see Joel's reaction and laughed. "You think I'm too old for this kind of thing?"

"Well, no. I..."

She patted him. "I was teasing."

Joel was relieved to find the picture so vital and good. Joel remembered Norman's new camera and when these pictures were taken, and thought that the man would now be his age, just past forty.

They went through the photographs together and then the drawings. They were fine, seen fully and rendered with immediacy and vitality. They were painfully rich with promise.

Joel said, "They're still awfully good. He had talent."

He stopped, wary of the pointless regret.

Meg asked, "You want them?"

"Yes."

"I'd like just one. I don't imagine I'll ever have the courage to hang it up, but I'd like to have it."

She pulled out a drawing, closed the portfolio, and began reknotting the ties, saying, "Let's just take these pictures and get the hell out of here."

They had lunch in Greenwich Village and then bought a mailing tube to put her drawing in. Joel took her to her train and waited with her till it was time for her to board.

He hugged and kissed her. She had to hurry to get her train, her stout figure bustling along, looking slightly comical. As he watched he was happy for the stab of affection he felt for her.

He hated going home to his empty apartment and wished desperately that Jerry weren't away. Well, he'd rent a movie, microwave something, fill the evening somehow.

It was after midnight when he turned the lights out and tried to get to sleep. Hopeless.

He got up, fetched the folder of pictures from the closet near the front door, and opened it. Looking at these pictures with Meg had been uncomfortable because he still found them erotic. Norman always said he didn't much like sex, so why were these pictures so laden with sensuality?

But his main reason for not wanting to look at

these pictures with Meg was that one of the drawings was of himself. Meg had either not recognized him or been discreet. He found the line drawing of himself. It was in black ink, with no shading, no color, just a supple, seemingly continuous line that shaped him lying nude, prone, his head twisted slightly toward the artist, the long hair he had worn at the time like a cape across his shoulders.

The drawing was beautifully done, and it made Joel angry. Norman was a goddamned fool. Norman had been the one people sought out and pursued, the one they coveted, wanted to do things for. Norman could have had anything. I was just the nice-looking guy with the nine-to-five. You know, Norman's roommate.

He looked at the drawing and wondered. Was his hair ever that black? Did he ever look that young and shy? How had Norman ever talked him into posing? They were old friends, but being drawn by Norman had felt as physically intimate as sex, and one just didn't have sex with old friends.

"This is embarrassing."

"This has nothing to do with friendship, Joel. You're just the subject, a thing. Stop twitching your shoulder."

"I'm uncomfortable. I've been here an hour."

"Think how happy Philip will be to have this."

"I'm not sure I'm going to see him anymore."

"Not again. You said he was the greatest thing that had ever happened to you."

"That was last week."

"Then I'll keep this for myself. This picture will be very valuable when I'm famous and you write my biography. An early Sullivan. My Nude Period. Dozens of nudes, just so when I'm old and famous they won't think that all I was interested in was art."

"Oh, God, don't talk about old. Bruce just turned thirty-five. I can't imagine being thirty-five."

"We'll be different. We'll stay beautiful, like Dorian Gray. I'll put this picture away and it will get old for you. You'll always look just the way you do now."

Norman stopped drawing and looked pensive. "I wish you could draw, Joel. Then you could draw me and keep my picture in the attic. We'd both look young and we could do anything we wanted and it would never show. The pictures could look like hell, but who'd care? I wouldn't give a damn, as long as all the really awful shit never got to me. I'm rotten at reality. What's so great about reality?"

Joel remembered that he had answered, "Not a thing I can think of. Can I get up for a while? This floor is hard. My balls are getting crushed."

He smiled at the picture of himself. It felt lovely to know he had been that handsome, to remember that there had been a time when there were no consequences, a time when there was nothing but more of everything ahead for him and his best friend.

ACTOR

I'd gone into Chock Full o' Nuts for a sandwich.
I've always loved their nutted cream cheese on raisin
bread. Anyway, I glanced up and saw this man. I
didn't want to stare, but I was struck by something. I
thought what an awfully good-looking man he'd be if
he took better care of himself. I was thinking about
him, so I looked up again and saw that I'd been looking in a mirror. I'd seen myself. It's not that I mind
encountering the great eternal verities, but I'd prefer
not to do it in Chock Full o' Nuts. I thought things
like that happened on mountaintops with heavenly
choirs on the sound track.

To be sure, I still looked good...just less good.

You see, it wasn't supposed to happen to me. I was
never going to get old, and there I was, a fast sixty.
Well, almost.

Actually, my birthday was the following week, and
Billy was giving me a party, about which I had very
mixed feelings. I also felt that they were all taking a
kind of malicious delight in announcing to all our

friends that I was over the hill. Hill, hell! I was over an alp. Billy said that when he carried my cake in, he wasn't going to sing "Happy Birthday." He was going to sing "The Old Gray Mare." I told him I hoped he looked good in cake.

I planned to go to the party after a day of facial massage and assorted treatments, and when they made their awful jokes about "getting on in years" I'd joke right back. Still, I wandered around regretting that I'd never lied about my age.

The party was one of Billy's specials, and Estelle's car was going to pick me up first and then we'd swing by and get her.

Estelle was my current "lady," as they're often called. A widow lady, actually. Her husband had been one of the great theater writers. He'd been dead for quite awhile, but his plays got done and done and done. There were constant first-class revivals all over the world, and Estelle was always running off somewhere to receive some honor in his memory. Within one month the Royal Shakespeare Company did one, and a month later Britain's National Theater did another, and then she went on to Munich, where they did the one about the newspaper business. They turned his plays into musicals, into television specials, and one even became a successful TV series. They were an annuity. Estelle didn't need an annuity.

Numerically, Estelle was seventh in a string of very nice women who seemed to keep coming into my life. They were always attached to the theater, and we always seemed to be able to put together some kind of arrangement that suited us both. To be clearer, we shared a bed from time to time, but we were always free.

I liked having the gals around because I liked parties and it was nice to be asked as a couple. No one was really fooled by these arrangements, but most people had something of the kind going on, so they turned it all into a little harmless gossip: I won't get stuffy about your whips if you'll lay off my hooker. That kind of thing.

When I wasn't with Estelle, I was still a desirable guest. Max Beerbohm said that the world is divided into only two groups, guests and hosts. I was a good guest. I was on Vogue's list of "ten most desirable male guests" four years running. That, dear boy, is the Oscar of the catering circuit.

With one exception, my ladies and I parted amicably enough when the time came and kept in touch and stayed friends. I even got out of a show and flew out to Hollywood when Sheila had her stroke. I stayed with her till she got back on her feet. Poor baby was ashamed to have me see her. The stroke got the right side of her face. Even with her hair draped down the side she couldn't hide it. Sad sight. She deserved better. After she got used to having me around, I told her to get her face out where I could see it and to stop turning away every time I came into her room. I told her, "You're going to have to look at someone, and you're going to have to learn to talk again. If you don't work, you'll die." She tried like hell. To tell the truth, it's no pleasure watching someone slobber or listening to them burble out their words, but that's the way it was. She got back almost all the use of her body. I used to get her laughing by telling her that she'd not only act again, she'd fuck again. She'd laugh and make the most awful noise. She's still around on television. Can't kill those old dames with a stick.

Anyway, Estelle was the latest, and she was going with me to my birthday party. While we were sitting in her limousine on the way to Billy's I thought, *Well, if you've got to head into senility, this is doing it in style.*

Billy threw a huge affair—there must have been eighty people. The guest list was "glittering," as the *Times* said.

Everybody was hugging everybody, so I hugged Robert, which made him break out in a cold sweat. Estelle said I was being mean.

Now here comes the big dramatic moment. Carl and Frederich came in with one of the most dazzling young men I'd ever seen. I knew the minute I saw him that he was either a model or an actor. Nobody else stands that way, always aiming at the key light. He was wasting his time, because he didn't *have* a bad angle. When Carl told me he was in *Hair*, I just nodded.

I've rarely been shy, but that young man made me feel very unsure of myself. He was attentive to the birthday boy, but I was intimidated by him. I'd been on the make too. I knew the pitch.

It was two or so when the car dropped me off at my apartment, and I was tired, so I was irritated when I got through the door and the phone was ringing. It was Craig, the young man from the party. He was in a phone booth on my corner and wanted to come up. I almost said no, but I said yes, and it was one of the worst nights of my life.

At sixty one likes to be ready for a gentleman caller.

I shouldn't try to make it funny. Actually, I was in a panic. You see, for the past few years, if I had a liaison... Jesus, I'm sounding like a prude. Let me start again.

For the last few years my tricks had been either hustlers or a few numbers from the old days. They suited me fine: no romance, no staying over, nothing too exhausting. and I always knew when they were to arrive, which gave me time to arrange myself, so to speak. I'd have time to get undressed and arrange the bedroom lights, like some kind of Colette heroine who's reached the age of high collars and pink scarves over the lamp shades. I'd meet my guest in the darkened hall and see him in. I wore a very full velvet robe. Then, while they were undressing, I'd drop my robe and hop into bed. I didn't like my body anymore. I'd look at it and think, *You need ironing.*

Did you see *A Little Night Music*? An older man has married a very young woman, who succeeds in remaining a virgin after the wedding. He sings about himself and there's a line that goes, "My body's all right / But not in perspective and not in the light." The audience laughed at the line while I just sat there nodding in agreement.

Craig was on his way up and, God help me, I wanted him. He was beautiful and I wanted him, even though I knew he had calculating eyes and that there was a price tag on him as surely as there was on any of those young men the service sent.

Craig finally rang the bell and I opened the door, and he stepped in and kissed me. He wasn't treading on virgin territory, but I went wobbly. He kept on kissing me and I kept thinking, *This is crazy and I should get him out.* But he said, "Let's go to bed," and I was too greedy to be sensible.

Well, he went to bed and I went into the bathroom. I hid the little telltale blue plastic box that holds my false teeth at night and I got out of my corset. I made the mistake of looking at myself in the mirror. The corset always left a reddish imprint around my middle. Every time I unwrapped myself I thought I looked as if I'd been made of wicker—the Wickerwork Man of Oz. There was a seed or something under my denture and they were beginning to bother me, and I was starting to cry. I couldn't expose myself to that beautiful boy. I couldn't let him put his tongue in my mouth and feel that plastic stuff that covered the roof of my mouth. I couldn't turn my head away from him and let him see the scars behind my ears from the lift.

I've no idea how long I was in there, but he called "Where are you?" and I yelled back, "Go home. Just go home."

He came into the bathroom and found me in my robe, sitting on the edge of the tub and crying. He never asked what was the matter. He just sat down next to me and put his arm around me until I calmed down.

I finally told him that my trouble was I wanted to be as young as he was. I wanted to be young again. I didn't want to be an old ruin with a lot of spare parts. Jesus, all I needed was a glass eye.

We went to bed because he wanted to and because I was exhausted by that time. He held me and soothed me, and I worried about the price.

We didn't make love until the next morning, and when we did it was extraordinary. It was as lovely as I remembered it being with Bernard in Catch Mills when I was a kid. That told me a lot I'd sooner not have known.

He called every day after that and kept saying he wanted to see me. I made up a lot of stories, and he told me he *would* see me again, so all I was doing was delaying things.

Have you ever made up your mind not to think about something? Then you know how successful that is.

I wouldn't think of Craig. I wouldn't think of him all the time.

I remember not liking *The Blue Angel* because I thought the Emil Jannings character was a silly old poop who deserved everything that happened to him. There was that old fool chasing after that German dumpling with fat thighs, and I hadn't the foggiest idea why he didn't pull himself together and just walk away. I didn't understand obsession because I'd never wanted anything that much.

I had a lunch date with Robert a few days later. Robert is not the kind of person in whom I confided, but he was handy that day and I was beside myself by then. I'd never been in love, and I had the awful feeling that I might be. I was too old for the grand passion. I still had a career to think about: my friends, Estelle, a lot of things. I thought I stood to lose a lot, and I couldn't think of one thing I'd be gaining. Life was very good as it was. Adding Craig to it could make it a mess.

Robert listened to my whole spiel and then said, "Do you feel you use Estelle?" I was outraged by his question, till I understood it. Estelle bought my clothes, took me on trips for months at a time, gave me entrée to any home in New York, or Palm Beach for that matter, and I never once felt that I'd used her. She didn't do anything for me I couldn't do for myself. I let her because she liked taking care of me.

I told Robert, "Of course I don't use her." He said, "Then what makes you think he'll use you? Besides," he said, "what makes you think this is the love of your life?" I said, "It is," and he said, "I hope not."

When Craig called again I made a date to see him. A date! At my age, a date.

Joe Allen's was a new spot then, a kind of poor man's Sardi's. It was lively, and we met there after he finished in *Hair*. He knew all the chorus people in Joe's and I knew all the character actors. That said a lot to me. When we'd finished our dinners he said, "We're going back to your place now." I thought he might say something like that, and I had a line ready that I'd been rehearsing since he called. I was simply going to say, "I'm too old for you." I fixed him with a very stern, no-nonsense look and said firmly, "You're too old for me." He roared, and I felt like an idiot. If I'd read my line right, it might have ended right there. I felt so silly that all my arguments were shot. He won that round. We went home.

He was charming, he was young, he was beautiful, he had talent, and he pursued me and I couldn't believe it. I didn't feel lucky, I felt afraid.

I didn't want to see *Hair*, but he insisted, so I took Estelle, who didn't want to see it either. Estelle was raised in Canada by Victorian parents, and this new kind of theater usually left her affronted and confused. Of course, we had house seats right down center in the orchestra. When a lot of the cast disrobed onstage I was startled. Estelle was genuinely shocked. Craig was one of the naked ones. He looked beautiful, and I realized that something awful had happened. I didn't want all those people gawking at him. He was mine. I didn't want to share him.

Have you ever been jealous? It's awful. It's unreasoning and destructive, and it went right to my stomach. It gave me the runs. Jealousy added a terrible burden to what I was already feeling, and I wanted to go someplace and hide. I didn't want all those feelings. I played a character once who was going through something of the same kind. He says, "I feel like I'm going sixty miles an hour and I want to jump, because I know that's safer than staying where I am." I jumped.

It was off-season, and I wasn't working just then, so I talked Estelle into a month in Mexico. I started avoiding Craig again. I stayed home a lot and stewed and sat on the john. He'd sounded irritated on the phone, but I wasn't sure it wasn't just acting. He must want something. The afternoon of the day before we were to leave, he called, and I told him I was going out of town for a month. He said he was coming right over, and I said he shouldn't.

He did, of course. I let him in but I couldn't look at him. He wanted to know what I was afraid of. I suppose I was feeling safe because I'd be far away in a few hours, so I told him that I was falling in love with him and I didn't want to. I didn't want to take the chance that I'd be used, I didn't want all those feelings, and I didn't want to feel jealous or worry that he'd still be young when I was using a wheelchair. I told him all that, everything I was afraid to say. If someone had said all that to me, I'd have left. He just sat there. I finally told him to get the hell out so I could have a good cry. I think I yelled at him.

He finally got up, but he went into the bedroom and just stayed in there.

I sat down. I was awfully tired. In all my life, I'd let people go when they were ready or I'd leave when I was. Never any fuss. I'd gotten to sixty without fuss. I sat there and knew that the person I wanted most in the world was in my bedroom. All I had to do was move. But that would take so much energy. I tried to outlast him. I thought that if I could sit there long enough he'd get up and go. I sat there and really prayed for God to send him away and leave me in peace.

I finally went. I went into the bedroom and took off my corset right in front of him. I hoped he'd be as repelled as I was ashamed. He just sat and watched. He didn't seem to notice that I was defying him to want me. Well, we made love.

Later I woke him up so he could go to the theater. He got up and dressed, and I just lay there. He came over and kissed me and said, "I want you to write to me." He seldom asked for anything. He just told me what he wanted. "Write to me." "I'm coming over." "Take me to the movies." "Come meet me." Well, why not?

I went to the door with him and said, "I love you," and he said, "Good," and left.

Estelle and I flew off the next morning. I'd finally surrendered, and I felt wonderful about that and terrible about leaving him. We went to Mexico City, which I've always loved, and so did Estelle. We had a lot of friends there and in Cuernavaca, so we were going all the time. I found some time almost every day to write Craig. I was in love and I was starting to enjoy it. I even started planning our future. I was going to play Henry Higgins. I would see that he got voice lessons with Fanny Bradshaw and acting classes with Hagen or Strasberg. I would introduce him to Alfred and Lynney and Helen and Noël and every name I thought worth dropping. I would take him to Shields for shirts and Dunhill for suits. To paraphrase Henry Higgins, I would heap the treasures of my Miltonic mind on the guttersnipe. I would do everything I was afraid he wanted me to do.

Of course, I had to try all of that to find out he didn't give a damn about any of it. He didn't want to get out of his dungarees or army jackets. He didn't

want to meet Noël Coward; he wanted to meet
Marlon Brando. I felt awful. If he didn't want what I
had to give, what the hell was he doing with me? Far
be it from me to accept the obvious.

And if he couldn't meet Brando, he'd settle for the
Beatles, all four of them. I didn't understand him. I'd
been crazy about the Boswell Sisters, but I never
cared to meet them, or the Mills Brothers, for that
matter.

Well, if I wasn't going to play Henry Higgins, who
could I play? I tried several Spencer Tracy roles on for
size and got no cooperation from Craig. I tried being
very "elder statesman," all compassionate understanding, until Craig asked me why I kept using "that funny
voice." I tried being the boulevardier, with absolutely
no success. Most of the time I felt like a cross between
Medea and King Lear, just another daffy jealous
queen screaming in the wilderness. I described myself
to Carl that way and he just nodded yes. You see, I
couldn't see myself as the young swain. I'd always
known who I was, and when I didn't I could fake it,
fall into some role and get through.

Every time I struck some pose, Craig would laugh
at me, or mimic me, which was even worse.

My friends took a very jaundiced view of the whole
affair. Carl told me that one couldn't get too early a
start on second childhood. Billy said it served me
right, which I never did understand, and Robert just
looked pruny. I was always grateful that none of that
lot took up theater criticism.

Well, anyway, I was happy when I wasn't too confused or jealous or crazy. Craig just moved into my life and stayed there.

I finally got used to having him around and started behaving naturally. My friends came to like Craig, or at least to accept him, even if grudgingly at first. I was careful not to introduce him to Estelle, but she noticed that I wasn't available all the time as I had been when I wasn't in a show.

Of course, when my friends started being comfortable with Craig, I became jealous of them all. I was sure that each of them was after Craig. If they joked with him, I was sure it was a pass. If they asked us to dinner, I was sure it was because they wanted to be near Craig. I think it's called paranoia. All that nonsense would go through my head and I'd listen to it and say to myself, *You're crazy, you've gone stark staring.*

But time cooled me down, and I started thinking that I had entirely too much time to think about myself—and about Craig—so I put myself out for work. I pestered my agent until he got me some readings.

Craig got offered a role in an off-Broadway play and decided to leave *Hair*. He'd been with it for nine months and was bored to death. He wasn't part of the original cast, and he had nothing to gain by staying with the show. I agreed. He should be doing a lot of different roles at his age. I read the play he'd been offered and thought it very good. I told him to accept.

He loved acting and worked hard. He apparently took direction without complaint, and when he talked to me about the show he sounded like a complete pro, a good sign. That pleased me. Early on I'd run lines with him, and I was happy to see that the play held up and got better with every reading. And he read well. All good signs. If the production was good, it would do very nice things for his career.

I took my agent—call him Pat—to opening night. Craig had third billing, and he was working with some awfully good people I knew either from their work or by reputation. It was a wonderful play and very well-directed, and Craig was awful. He'd read well with me, but he washed out onstage. He was even technically bad. He swallowed the ends of lines, and his gestures never matched up with what he was saying...like Nixon. He was awkward and amateurish, and my heart went out to him.

I thought that perhaps I was being too demanding because of my own ego. I wanted so much to be proud of him. Before I went backstage I asked Pat what he thought. He asked me if I wanted the truth, and I told him I certainly did. Pat was kind and sensible. He said he'd been around too long to dismiss any talent on the basis of one performance, but that Craig lacked so much in basic technique that it was hard to tell.

I'd always been able to go backstage and tell the most outrageous lies to friends. You know the kind of thing: Darling, I was simply swept off my feet. You've never been better or prettier—or handsomer—or whatever.

Oh, God, how I didn't want to go backstage. I wanted to lie to Craig—and knew I'd botch it. I didn't know what to do, so I asked Pat. "Well," he said, "if he loves the theater, tell him to get to work. If you want to help, get him to the best people."

I decided to split the difference. I would lie back-stage and save the truth for later when I'd had a chance to do a bit of scripting. I wasn't going to damage his ego for anything in the world, but I didn't want him to go pointlessly on telling everyone he was an actor and never working or working on junk. I'd seen too much of that in my time.

But when you come right down to it, who was I to be ladling out that kind of judgment? I don't know how to make this clear.

Most actors go into that business because they love it. Not *love* like "I love that hat" or "I loved that show" but love the way a lot of people love power or money. You don't get up at nine in the morning for the salary, you give your life to it. To my loss, I never did, so I never went much beyond being an able journeyman. But I knew the goods when I saw it, and I saw it often, and I knew what it cost the people who did it. I think acting may be the toughest and worst bargain a person can make in life. If you make that bargain, there's often no way out. I've watched people leave the business, and the luster goes off them, their souls become cautious. And if you think I'm being too dramatic, get to know some actors.

I prayed for conviction to make lying to Craig convincing, but I didn't get it.

I went backstage and used an evasion. I said, "It was wonderful to see you up there. You looked terrific." And we all went off to the cast party to wait for the reviews: I didn't stay till they came in. I told Craig to get drunk or high or whatever and to have a wonderful time. I fled. I felt like Judas.

The show came off pretty well, but Craig was slaughtered by the reviewers. I don't remember the adjectives, but they were harsh. It was after two when he called me in tears. I told him to come along and I'd give him a drink he obviously didn't need.

When he got there I was surprised to see that he wasn't nearly as drunk as I'd thought. So I sat him down and decided to get him really pissed.

But I wasn't going to get off with a drink and a pat on the head. He asked me if I'd tell him the truth about his performance. I honestly told him I wasn't sure I could or even should, and I could see him stiffen. *Well,* I thought, *in for a penny, in for a pound.*

I brought him a drink and sat near him. I started with the longest, most rambling preamble you've ever heard, and he knew I was dodging. I knew he knew, so I stopped and started again. I told him that I wanted to help him get the best help possible, people to work with him, so that he could work on his voice and technique. I told him I didn't know how much talent he had. I knew he had the dedication. I finally told him that he hadn't held his own on that stage that night.

And he said, "And I suppose all that work you want me to do will make me a great star and brilliant actor like you?" He said, "If I get to act like you after forty years, I don't want it."

That hurt some—that hurt a lot—but I let it go. He

went on about my acting until I had to tell him to shut up.

He wanted to fight with me. I didn't have the heart for it. I'd told him the truth; I'd taken a terrible chance and lost. I told him that, and that he'd have to make what he wanted of it, but he must never ask me for the truth again if all he wanted was some god-damned lie that could damage any chance he had to become good.

He told me to go fuck myself and who did I think I was and that I could shove it, and he left.

I sat there feeling lousy and wishing I'd lied even if he hadn't believed it.

There were several weeks of silence after that.

They managed to get another week out of the show, but there was paper for it everywhere. Sad. It was a good play, but that was one of those seasons when if it wasn't British and it was serious, you could forget it. We didn't know any of the same people, so I didn't hear a word about Craig. I eventually got a card from Florida that simply said "I'm here for a while" and was signed with just his initials.

I cried a lot, and my friends got heartily fed up with my carrying-on. I was grateful for Estelle and the parties, and I went back to being with her a lot of the time. I read for some more shows and actually went into rehearsal for one until their backing dried up. I did a lot of entertaining and had people by two or three times a week; mostly other actors, with some friends mixed in. I've always needed a lot of people around. I think it's because I grew up in a large family. Carl says it's because I need an audience.

When I was alone in the apartment I hated it. Craig had given me a hi-fi, on which he'd constantly played stuff I couldn't stand, and when that wasn't on, the television he'd talked me into buying was going. I'd never much liked radio, and I was afraid I liked television too much. I liked game shows. The more awful something was, the more I seemed to like it, so I never turned it on. I was embarrassed by my own taste.

I finally got an offer to go out for six months with a good production of *Desk Set,* so I took it. My old chum Anita was going to star. The older ladies liked doing it. They could be romantic in it without looking silly.

I didn't get used to Craig's being gone, but I didn't stop living. It gave me time to think, not that I needed time to think about becoming sixty-one.

We were in rehearsal over at Broadway Arts when he came back. He was waiting outside the studios, and when I came out he just walked up to me and said, "Take me to dinner."

He looked awful. I didn't ask him where he'd been or what he'd been doing. In a way, it was none of my business, and I didn't want it to be. It wasn't that I didn't care. By the time we'd finished dessert I'd told him about the show and our itinerary, which was Boston, Chicago, Denver, and San Francisco, and I'd told stories about the cast. I ran out of conversation. He finally said something like "Find me the right teachers."

I was very out of touch with who was a good

teacher, so I told him he was in a better position to find good teachers than I was but that I'd help him in every way possible. But he said he wanted me to tell him. I said that a lot of the young people I admired had some training at RADA, the Royal Academy of Dramatic Arts in London. And he said, "Can you help?" I said, "Maybe," because I had a lot of connections over there, and I'd even ask Estelle to help if I had to.

When we left the restaurant he said, "Take me home," and I said no. He didn't argue. I had to give him some money for a hotel, but I couldn't take him home with me. I couldn't tell if he was angry or hurt about my saying no. I didn't even know what I was feeling.

Then he scared the hell out of me by grabbing me and kissing me right on the lips out in front of the restaurant. I didn't even dare look around to see who might have seen us, I just bolted off down the street. He'd kissed me in front of God and everybody and scared me. All I could think was, *Maybe people thought we were Italian.* Somehow I felt that half of New York had been there watching. I'd been kissed in the street, right on the lips. I'd be arrested. When I finally slowed down I started to laugh. For some reason, I felt good.

So I walked home, explaining Craig to myself for the nine millionth time. He was out of the question. He was too young. I was too old for all the drama. When he'd just taken off I'd pulled things together again, but I swore I would not go through that again. I had no intention of being a professional old fool.

Well, I'd said it all to myself so often I was thoroughly bored with it. And it was hard to concentrate because I kept thinking of the kiss. What would people say?

It was early when I got in, so I called around to see who was free. Billy had had a date cancel on him, so I met him at East Five Five, a classy gay restaurant where everybody gathered to show off a new costume or a new lover or some new money. Billy met me at the bar and asked me what had run over me. I told him Craig was back and he said, "And?" I said, "And nothing." I told Billy I planned to help Craig out with his studies and then I went on about my age, his age, his needs, my fears. Billy listened as long as he could and then he said, "Do it or don't, but make up your mind." I asked him what he'd do, and he said, "I'd either have some fun with it or give it up." He wouldn't agonize over it. I said I was too old, and Billy fixed me with that beady eye of his and said, "No, my love, you're not as young as you want to be, and there's a difference." He finally said, "You're not going to get many more chances for anything, so I'd take it."

There's some truth for you.

We got swacked and sentimental and talked about old times, which usually bores the hell out of both of us. Billy had to put me in a cab.

Craig woke me up in the middle of the night. He was crying. I don't remember him saying a thing on the phone, just crying. Well, you can guess the rest. Come home to Papa, come home to the old fool, come home to the old fart.

I finally had to ask Estelle's help to get him into

RADA in midterm, but she brought it off through one of those "theater Sir" friends of hers. She was very curious about my interest in the "young man," as she constantly called him, and I was evasive enough to make her even more interested.

Craig left for England a couple of days after arrangements were complete, and that left me with three days to pack myself up for my tour. We planned to meet in England when my tour was over. I'd fly from San Francisco.

My tour ended in Denver. I came to in the Denver hospital, and there was Estelle way off in the distance. She said I asked her to get Craig, and when she said she didn't know how to reach him I apparently cursed her out for losing him. And that is how I returned to life. I'd been out for two days.

I remember running to center stage for the curtain call and that was it. Perfect blackout, till Estelle.

We were doing nice business in Denver. Anita had a following and her fans always turned out. We were all feeling the altitude, and one martini worked like two. We had to rest a lot because *Desk Set* is played at a pretty fast pace. But we were adjusting. I'd been complaining to the stage manager that he'd have to carry me on for my last scene, but I whizzed through it and stood in the wings for the curtain line. It came, and I moved to my position for the call, and the curtain went up on me lying flat-out center stage. You don't need an exit line if you've got a really great bit of business. They told me Anita was so surprised, she went right ahead and took her bow as if I weren't there. She had the grace to take only one bow. I almost died to do it, but I finally upstaged her.

They got me into intensive care and kept me under with drugs. Thank God it was Saturday night when it happened, because they had till Monday night to get my standby up in the part. Anita called Estelle, who flew out to make arrangements to have my body shipped back east. It was that close.

When they started cutting back on drugs and I got my wits back, I found out I'd had a heart attack and a fairly major one. Since I wasn't dead, I didn't pay much attention to the details. I think I felt a little cheated that I didn't make my final exit onstage. If you die in bed, there's no drama, nothing to talk about. If you do it center stage, it becomes part of the lore.

When I left intensive care, Estelle had me put into one of the hospital's best private rooms, and she saw to necessities like vodka and Pepperidge Farm cookies.

I'd been in that room a couple of days when I woke up in the middle of the night and felt that there was someone in the room. It was Craig. I asked him how he'd gotten there, and he said Carl had reached him and arranged for tickets back. I'd talked to Carl and Billy and Robert every day, and no one had said a word. I told them I planned to wait till I was out of the hospital to tell Craig.

Craig asked me how bad it was, and I told him that I was a lot better and might even go back to the show in San Francisco. That's what I'd been thinking. Craig was the fifth person who told me I was crazy.

Craig said he was going to take me back to New

York and look after me, and I told him to stay a day or so and then get his ass back to RADA. He just looked at me and said, "I found out I'm not good enough." He said it was OK, that he'd actually felt relief once he knew for sure. He'd never worry that he hadn't given it his best try. It must have hurt like hell when he found out. He looked fine, so I didn't pursue it. He always looked thc way he felt.

Estelle met Craig the next day. She couldn't have been nicer to him. When she told him she knew he'd help me get better faster, I knew I didn't have any secrets from her. Ladies in their sixties are adaptable. The two of them would hang around my room while I had my gruel and Jell-O, then they'd go off and gorge themselves at Brown's or somewhere.

I started feeling well enough to become a pain in the ass about getting out and joining the company in San Francisco. That's when Estelle told me I was obviously well enough to be told that I'd been replaced. Estelle said it was her doing. She'd connived with Anita to remove that temptation by putting someone good in the part.

That's when Estelle told me what was going to be done. I'd be let out of the hospital to go home by train. She and Craig would travel with me. The doctors had told her that I was to do no stage work until the doctor in New York gave his approval, and she said, "Frankly, that may never be." All I could think to say was, "Oh!" She saved the best till last: Estelle said she wanted to marry me, and I blurted out, "But I don't love you," and she was very annoyed and she asked me what that had to do with anything at our age. She said she'd never known a man she enjoyed more and that she wanted to take care of me. God knows she could and often did.

I told her I wanted to think about it. I still wince when I think of my end of that conversation; my lines were right out of reel five of a Betty Grable movie. Can you imagine? "I want to think about it." Heroine drops curtsy and exits.

Estelle told me to take my time but that there was one other think she wanted to say. She said, "I want to marry you, but no little boys." I didn't have a line for that. She said she liked Craig but she wanted to preclude gossip and she had no intention of being laughed at because her husband dallied. She knew what our crowd could say about one another. It could be pretty funny and pretty ugly. Estelle has never deserved slander.

I told her I understood. I also understood how kindly she meant her proposal. I wanted to tell her about Craig. I wanted to tell her that I loved him, but I was afraid she'd just make a sour face or, worse yet, laugh at me. Knowing her, she probably wouldn't have done either, but I was afraid.

Nothing more was ever said about the matter. I didn't say no and she didn't ask again. We stayed the best of friends. I loved her, but marriage wouldn't have done much for us. Besides, I'd kept proving I didn't want to be without Craig. I'd finally given in.

Craig left the train in Chicago and flew on ahead to New York to be sure the apartment was in shape and that the hospital bed we'd ordered had arrived.

Craig and I settled in. He looked after me and I got well. I got up, I went shopping, I started going back to doing some entertaining, and I started wanting to work. All I was afraid of was sex. Craig kept making overtures and I'd be evasive. I wanted him badly, but I was afraid of dropping dead on him. The idea that one will pop off in mid ejaculation puts a certain damper on one's ardor. I kept having visions of the whole ghastly event. I'd learned that my life was taking a fairly ironic turn. I'd faced my age in Chock Full o' Nuts, I'd had my only proposal in a hospital room, and I was sure I would die in flagrante delicto.

I'm happy to report, Craig finally seduced me. He got me drunk, and I have absolutely no sense when I'm drunk. You'd have to be drunk to risk your life for a fuck. Of course he got to use the amyl nitrite the doctor prescribed for me.

I'd started feeling a lot better, so I tried getting some television commercial work. I figured they wouldn't overtax and the extra money would be nice. I did two commercials, and I completely enjoyed making them. I just hated seeing them. In one I was a titled Englishman, and I was next to a Russian wolfhound in a two-shot as I said, "I put on the dog at the kennel club because of what I put into Czar." Then the dog said, "Ralston." In the other one I was an army general bending over a map and saying "Capture their appetite with Stouffer's." I hated the kidding I got. People were always quoting them to me or making lame jokes. They'd come to table at our apartment, and when I'd serve the entrée someone would say something like "Oh, good, Wes's famous Ralston ragout." I decided I could do without that kind of work.

I don't know how to describe my life with Craig. It wasn't exciting or hilarious, and there are almost no good stories. It was actually a little humdrum, and it suited me. And Craig was happy. He lost that restless tic in his nature.

Much to everyone's surprise, Craig and I turned out to be good for each other. However, our first Christmas together he bought me love beads and I gave him a Sulka tie. As you can see, there was something of a gap. But we wore each other's gifts like good little soldiers. He took me to Fire Island that summer and I took him to Venice and Florence. Craig got me to let my hair grow. But I had it cut after Carl said I looked like Wallace Beery playing Rapunzel. We both tried pot. (Craig became withdrawn and depressed, and I tried to go out our tenth-floor window. It didn't suit us.) We've been together quite awhile now. I've watched Craig go from shopping at army surplus stores to the Chemise Lacoste counter at Bloomingdale's. Well, it's to be expected. He's getting older.

We adjusted to each other. My hardest adjustment was to letting him have his little flings on the side. I didn't so much adjust as learn to keep my trap shut. As my ma used to say, "Least said, soonest mended."

I'd do some traveling with Estelle in the winter, Craig and I would go to Europe with friends in the spring or fall, and there were usually summers at Fire Island: a good life.

I was able to buy this apartment with Robert's help—and Estelle's. Estelle even started including Craig in some of her parties, and I taught him which flatware was used with what.

Craig held some jobs, and he'd stay as long as he was happy in them or until we felt like going away for a while. It was selfish of me. I wanted him with me as much as possible. I didn't much want to be alone. Besides, I loved the time I spent with him. My friends didn't approve. Carl said, "You know, Craig's not dumb." Billy said Craig should have some kind of career. Leave it to Robert to tie the whole thing up. Robert said, "What kind of life is he going to have after you're gone?"

That was plain enough. He was right, and that got him the anger he deserved. Robert could put up with my irritation because he was right. I'd seen it often enough in New York. There was that movie executive who'd been living with a lover for over thirty years when he died. In less than a day the family moved in and the lover was on the street. They even kept his clothes. I'd seen a lot of variations on that story.

But I didn't want my friends to be right. I was being selfish, but that's never stopped me. I wanted my time with Craig. We'd lived together six years by then.

Robert and Billy worked out a scheme. The trust Teddy had left me couldn't be touched, but it could make investments if they looked safe. So Billy said he would open a retail outlet for his products and Robert would partially finance it from the trust. Some kind of stock setup. Craig would manage it and be given a salary and a chance to get stock and a permanent spot in Billy's corporation. It was somewhat more complicated than that, but that's the gist.

Craig started working, and he loved it. He helped design the shop, got very involved, was away a lot, and I resented it. But it would make Craig self-sufficient, and I couldn't argue.

Of course, I started getting itchy with all that time on my hands. I'd lost my playmate. Carl kept saying he could get me some TV work if I wanted, but I'd never really liked television work.

Without really noticing, I guess I'd retired. I was genuinely surprised when I realized that. I was really out of things by then. My agent had retired and I'd lost all my work contacts, and besides, if I got a job I'd have to give up watching *All My Children.*

I ran into an old chum at one of Estelle's parties. He was a very big man on Broadway and he'd directed a movie or two. He asked me if I'd be interested in reading for a part in a new show he was doing. I almost said, "I don't *read.*" Instead, I just said thank you. He sent the script over and, as he said, it was a small part but very flashy. I checked with my doctor and Craig, and ended up getting the part. Any lingering image of glamour I might have had was about to go down the drain. I had one scene in the second act. I played the lead's father, and my son has asked me over for dinner. My costume was out of some second-hand store—trousers bagged, the crotch around my ankles, the belt seven inches too big, shirt unpressed. I stooped, I shuffled, I gummed, I acted my age. In the play my son has asked me over because he feels guilty about neglecting me. My son is between wives, his current affair is a mess, and he can't seem not to make more and more money. I knew my son was trying to buy off his conscience with me and I wouldn't let him. I'd always picked up my marbles, and I'd raised him that way too. In the scene I got to be angry and high-minded and feisty and lovable, all in ten minutes. I end up near the door ready to leave, and I say, "You must have been very lonely to have invited me over. I didn't come because I was lonely. All I've gotten for my trouble is a lecture on what a rotten father I was. Well, I haven't been your father for twenty-five years— not since you left us. If you fuck up now, you do it on your own. Don't blame me. I'm too busy for you. I'm busy with what's left. Don't you dare come to my funeral and cry over me. I don't want you there. You're not my son anymore. You're what you've made yourself and I don't like you."

Exit. Applause.

I never left that stage without a big hand. I never took my solo curtain call without getting a rise in applause. I wasn't able to stay with the show too long, but it got me a Tony nomination. I didn't win, but not bad for someone who was seventy. I still knew my craft.

I did the movie too. It's nice to have that around to look at. I'm proud of it. I got the best reviews I've ever had. Craig prefers my old RKO movies. I look at them and can't remember playing any of the scenes, but I remember all that happened off-camera. I remember the jokes and the horseplay and who was sleeping with whom. There's not a reason in the world to remember any of the lines.